THE PERNICIOUS PROPOSAL

Caroline did not hesitate when Patrick Danvers made his proposal of marriage. "No," she said. "I have not the least intention of selling my person for dresses and pin money. Now if you will excuse me."

But Patrick refused to move aside. "You would not find it an unpleasant experience, I think," he murmured. Then, to her utter horror, he grasped her shoulders, and before she realized his intent, he bent his head to hers. It was her first real kiss.

Resolutely, she stiffened, and pushed him away. He released her abruptly. "Your pardon, Miss Ashley—I should not have done that."

"I should think it all of a piece," she choked when she found her voice. " 'Tis expected of Devil Danvers!"

But what Caroline had not expected—though she did not say so—was what this devilish kiss had done to her. . . .

A Signet Super Regency

"A tender and sensitive love story . . . an exciting blend of romance and history"
—*Romantic Times*

The
Guarded
Heart
Barbara
Hazard

Passion and danger embraced her—
but one man intoxicated her flesh
with love's irresistable promise . . .

Beautiful Erica Stone found her husband mysteriously murdered in Vienna and herself alone and helpless in this city of romance . . . until the handsome, cynical Owen Kingsley, Duke of Graves, promised her protection if she would spy for England among the licentious lords of Europe. Aside from the danger and intrigue, Erica found herself wrestling with her passion, for the tantalizingly reserved Duke, when their first achingly tender kiss sparked a desire in her more powerfully exciting than her hesitant heart had ever felt before. . . .

DEVIL'S MATCH

Anita Mills

A SIGNET BOOK

NEW AMERICAN LIBRARY

Copyright © 1987 by Anita Mills

SIGNET TRADEMARK REG.U.S.PAT. OFF. AND FOREIGN COUNTRIES
REGISTERED TRADEMARK—MARCA REGISTRADA
HECHO EN CHICAGO, U.S.A.

SIGNET, SIGNET CLASSIC, MENTOR, ONYX, PLUME,
MERIDIAN and NAL BOOKS are published by NAL PENGUIN
INC., 1633 Broadway, New York, New York 10019

First Printing, November, 1987

1 2 3 4 5 6 7 8 9

PRINTED IN THE UNITED STATES OF AMERICA

DEVIL'S MATCH
is dedicated to
the memory of my mother,
NELLIE BROWN.

Her pride in my accomplishments
was a reflection of her love.

1

The solicitor cleared his throat and began reading the last will and testament of the late Viscount Westover. Of those assembled in the dark and gloomy Westover library, all but one hung on every word. The exception, the titular heir, appeared detached from the proceeding and quite impervious to the frequent glances of acute dislike cast his way. Not that the others believed that he could possibly be disinterested, for the late Vernon Danvers had cut up quite warm if the truth were known—so warm, in fact, that the fortune was reputed to be an enormous one hundred thousand pounds at the least.

Having read the customary introductory passages about the state of the departed viscount's mental health, the solicitor paused to peer dramatically over the top of his half-spectacles at the group. It was clear that he was enjoying their impatience before he finally deigned to continue in stentorian accents with, "To my sister Lenore, I bequeath the sum of two thousand pounds that she may continue in her support of worthy and charitable causes."

All eyes turned toward that lady as the entire assemblage suppressed grins at the viscount's final gesture toward his cold and greedy sister. Even her brother Hugh covered a smile and nodded in appreciation since it was well-known that Lenore Canfield had never willingly given anyone anything of value in her life. As for the lady herself, she colored uncomfortably, but bit back her customary sharp retort.

"And to my brother Hugh," the solicitor resumed, "the sum of two thousand pounds to be used for the good of his parish . . ."

It was Hugh Danvers' turn to receive the stares of his unsympathetic relations. Red-faced, he started from his seat in protest, but then thought better of a public display of avarice. After all, as a man in holy orders, it was unseemly to reveal his desire for worldly rewards.

"To my nieces Vivian and Charlotte, I leave one thousand pounds each for any purpose they may choose. Since it appears unlikely at this date that either will ever wed, I recommend it as a source of independence for them both . . ."

"Why, that old nip-cheese!" one of them gasped. "A paltry thousand! 'Tis most unfair!"

"Hush, Charlotte," cautioned her sister. "We have not heard it all."

"To my nephews Charles, Lawrence, and Quentin Danvers, I bequeath one thousand pounds each in the hopes that they will learn to conserve their substance before it is too late. If, at the end of one year, the sum inherited remains intact, it shall be doubled."

"I say . . . I object!" A sartorially splendid young man lurched to his feet, his face livid above his high, stiffly starched collar points. "He cannot have meant it!"

"Poor Charlie," his brother Lawrence clucked in mock commiseration, "I daresay you'll have to pay the tradesmen now or leave the country. You've put them off for years with your expectations, haven't you?"

"But it ain't right! The old fellow had a hundred thousand if he had a farthing! I agree with Charlotte—'tis paltry!"

"Leave him be, Larry," Quentin cut in sharply. "It ain't like you can stand for it, either, is it? I mean, your thousand won't last you a week in the gaming hells you frequent. At least I shall see mine doubled."

"Quen—"

"Tut-tut," came the languid voice from the depths of the overstuffed chair in the back of the room. Almost in unison, everyone turned toward the acknowledged black sheep of the family. Lounging easily against the button-tufted leather, the young gentleman appeared unconcerned with the dismay of the others as he vaguely waved a fine Belgian linen handkerchief in the solicitor's direction. "Pray proceed, sir," he directed, "that I may be on the road before 'tis dark."

"Coming it too strong, Patrick," Lawrence retorted. "Let us see if you are so smug when 'tis told what pittence he's left you."

The young man straightened himself in his chair and lifted an eyebrow while murmuring, "How kind of you to concern yourself for me, Larry, but I assure you that I am not likely to be disappointed in the least. After all, I never expected anything of the old man when he was alive, and I certainly expect nothing now." He managed a brief, wry smile that did not begin to reach his very fine hazel eyes. "And lower expectations lead to fewer disappointments, one must admit."

"Ahem!" the solicitor cleared his throat loudly. "Now, sirs, if I may proceed, after all—"

"But I believe that I have already directed you to do so," the young man reminded him, and settled back in his seat.

Weatherby cast a wary eye in his direction and then hastened through the reading. "As for my nephew Patrick Danvers," he intoned, "it has been discovered to me at considerable expense that since Patrick is the son of my next brother, there is no means of preventing his succession to my title, despite how abhorrent that circumstance is to me . . ." The plump, balding man paused for a nervous glance at the gentleman in question before plunging on, "For in the five years since his majority, I am persuaded that he has left no vice undiscovered. Having brought disgrace and dishonor on this family, he is now its titular head, a singular injustice that must nonetheless be borne." Again, Weatherby looked up for some sign of the legendary temper and was relieved to see Patrick still in his chair.

"Do go on," the young man prompted almost lazily, "for now you have reached the point that interests me."

"Uh . . . yes . . . well . . ." The solicitor's discomfort seemed to increase as he pulled at his cravat, cleared his throat, and took a deep breath before screwing his courage to the sticking point and reading anew. "However," he continued finally, "since I find I am unable to dispose of my title as I would, I deem it necessary to provide for its maintenance on condition. Therefore, I leave the remainder of the estate, all lands and monies not specifically bestowed elsewhere, to Patrick—"

There was a collective gasp of shock and outrage from every relative but Patrick. He sat still as stone, his face set and inscrutable, while Weatherby finished, "—on condition that he marry a female of respectable birth and unimpeachable virtue and give evidence of producing a more suitable son within the twelvemonth of this reading. To provide for him during this time, he shall have at his disposal the sum of ten thousand pounds to settle on the unfortunate lady. Should he prove unwilling or unable to meet the stipulations set herein, the money will revert, in its entirety, to be used for the establishment of a school for indigent but able boys under the direction of Mr. Jonas Weatherby."

Not daring to look again at Patrick, the solicitor enumerated various small bequests of articles and pensions to the Westover retainers. He was wasting his breath, however, as no one in the room was now listening. To a person, they stared at Patrick, their faces mirroring the revulsion and indignation that each felt at the perceived injustice of it all. As for Patrick himself, his only reaction was a barely discernible twitch of the muscles of his jaw.

Hugh Danvers, his face mottled a dangerous purplish-red, found his voice and spat out, "You! 'Tis outside of enough! His entire fortune indeed!" Shaking uncontrollably, he raised a blunt finger to point accusingly at his nephew. "He cannot have been of sound mind, I tell you—not after what you have done to this family!"

"Uncle Hugh, calm yourself!" Vivian implored as she caught at his arm. "He's not worthy of an apoplectic fit—he's not! And besides," she added in a reasonable tone, "he'll not spend a farthing above the ten thousand, Uncle, for there's not a respectable female as would have him." Favoring the new viscount with a contemptuous glance, she sniffed, "No one would consider Patrick an eligible connection!"

"But what use is that to us, pray?" Lawrence complained. "As I heard it, there's precious little of Uncle Vernon's money that any of us'll see."

"Aye—this time next year, the whole bloody fortune will be building a damned school," Quentin snorted.

Seemingly unperturbed by the ire of his relations, the object of their disaffection unfolded his tall frame from the depths of his chair and stood, his attention absorbed with the removal of a small nub of lint from the sleeve of his perfectly tailored blue superfine coat. Then, adjusting the same sleeve down over a decidedly masculine wrist, he reached gracefully to retrieve his hat from the nearby table.

His face was schooled into bland amiability, but there was that about him which gave even his most disapproving critics pause. It was difficult to describe—not that they had not tried, of course, for more than once his Aunt Lenore could have been heard to remark out of his hearing that "Patrick is but an impeccably polite savage, if the truth dare be told." Not that this was readily apparent even to an interested observer, for a cursory appraisal of the young man would reveal rather an extraordinarily handsome fellow whose striking good looks came from a perfectly chiseled face, hair the color of polished mahogany, almost hypnotic hazel eyes whose color altered to reflect his thoughts, and an excellently fleshed frame whose proportions were a delight to Stultz, his fashionable tailor. Yet there was something to be sensed rather than seen in Patrick Danvers, an unstudied, almost feline grace that combined with a certain air of self-assurance to evoke a sense of danger in his presence. No—there was something beneath that controlled facade. Even when he had been sent down from Oxford for his first duel, it was acknowledged that he was more distinguished than most of his peers in his studies, a thoughtful but incisive scholar of the classics, in fact. Indeed, he had even been immensely popular with his fellows and his relatives, in sharp contrast to the dislike he evoked now. But he'd earned a reputation as a duelist, something which of itself could have been easily forgiven but for his failure to follow the accepted rules. Yet twice, when he should have fled the country to avoid prosecution for fatal duels, he had chosen to remain and face public inquests which, while eventually exonerating him, nonetheless had exposed his ancient and noble family to disgrace—an unpardonable sin in the eyes of the *haut ton*.

Unwilling to let him go quietly, Quentin could not resist taunting him, "Well, Coz, you can whistle that fortune down the wind, can't you? I'd say the old man has had his final revenge—all that money dangling in front of you and you cannot get it."

"Well, I should hope not!" Vivian added maliciously. "Not after what he did!"

"Aye," Charles joined in, "Pat, I'll lay you a monkey that says you cannot meet the terms."

"Of course he cannot," Lady Lenore sniffed, "but what comfort is that to us, pray?" Ignoring the new

Lord Westover, she turned to the others. "I say that once he is gone, we must put our heads together with Mr. Weatherby to determine just how this infamous document may best be circumvented."

"Oh, Aunt Lenore—do you truly think it possible?" Charlotte breathed. "I cannot bear that it should go to Patrick. Besides," she added with feeling, " 'tis not right the way Uncle Vernon positively encouraged us to toady to him in expectation and then to make no provision—"

"Charlotte!" Vivian reproved hastily. "We did not toady—we merely paid him his due when he was alive."

The new viscount observed the hope mirrored on his relatives' faces as they contemplated the prospect of cutting him out of the family fortune. For a brief moment his hazel eyes exposed the pain and anger he felt, and then they were veiled as he turned to Charles.

"A monkey, Charlie?" he asked with deceptive softness. "Do you not think that a poor wager, given the stakes? But if you will make it your thousand pounds, you are on."

"Don't do it, Charlie," Quentin warned. "Remember what happens to those foolish enough to gamble with him."

"Aye," Larry agreed, "ten to one, you'd not live to collect it."

Shrugging, Patrick reached into his coat pocket to draw out a slender leather pouch. Opening it, he extricated a sheaf of banknotes and extended them toward his uncle. "I believe you'll find a thousand there, Uncle Hugh, but I suggest you count it out in front of Charlie to be sure. Now"—he turned back to his cousin—"do you cover it or not?"

For an instant, Charles met his eyes and then looked away. "At what odds?" he asked with a dry mouth.

"Perfectly even. A bargain for you, wouldn't you say? You could have three thousand at year's end, after all."

Charles hesitated. "I . . . I'd not live to spend it."

"My dear Charles, even I should scarce be able to murder you outright," Patrick reminded him. "You'd have to agree to meet me first."

"Remember Bridlington and Haworth," Lawrence cautioned his brother. "He's as good as there is with a pistol."

"And with a sword," Quentin threw in.

"May the Lord forgive you all," Hugh Danvers intoned sanctimoniously, "for gambling on this sad occasion. Our time would be better spent listening to Lenore. And I am not entirely averse to allowing Patrick to participate in circumventing this outrageous instrument."

"Alas"—Patrick shook his head to decline—" 'tis scarcely to my benefit. After all, I seem to be the principal heir."

"Only if you wed a respectable female and get yourself an heir of your own," Charlotte gibed indelicately. "And none of us thinks you can do it."

"Well, Charlie?"

Charles Danvers wavered and then nodded. "Aye. Weatherby, you can give my thousand to Uncle Hugh to hold. But I warn you," he addressed Patrick, "that I ain't going to be called out for nothing! I may be the slowtop of this family, but I ain't a fool."

"Well, if that's settled then . . ." Patrick pushed back a stray lock of dark red hair and set his hat at a decidedly rakish angle. Flashing his most engaging grin at his outraged relations, he executed a mocking bow. "As we are agreed on the wager, I really must be getting on. Quite sorry to be leaving my charming family, of course," he apologized, "but since none of you appears marriageable in the least, I shall bid you all good day." Catching sight of Charlotte's totally indignant scowl, he favored her wickedly. "Sorry, my dear, but I fear we should not suit at all."

"Well, I never!" she sputtered to his back. "As if I'd have you! I'd die on the shelf first!"

As he let himself out the door, he could hear Vivian soothing her sister with, "Hush, dearest—'tis but his hateful tongue." His anger seemed to mount in direct proportion to his descent down the portico steps until he shouted to his waiting driver and coachman, "You may ride inside—I'll take the ribbons myself!"

They looked at each other, exchanging glances of trepidation, before Barnes, the driver, moved to vacate the box. Grimacing, he muttered under his breath to the coachy, " 'Tis the devil's ride ter town, by the looks o' hit."

"Aye, but oo's ter blame 'im, wot wi' 'em Friday-faces," Rogers hissed back as he clambered after "Messel'—jest wisht they was ridin' wi' 'im."

His jaw set, his eyes dark with anger, Patrick heaved himself up into the box. Tossing his hat under the seat, he loosened his cravat and unbuttoned his coat before taking the reins. There would be a headwind and it looked like rain, but he meant to make good time back to London in spite of it. Flicking the whip to crack above his horses, he hunched forward in the seat as the coach lunged forward, threw the hapless occupants back against their seats, and picked up speed.

He was furious with his family and even more furious with himself. He ought not to have come at all, he knew, but he had—and look what it had got him! Certainly not the least goodwill from them—quite the opposite, in fact. Damn his Uncle Vernon! Could he not have forgiven a boy's hotheaded lapses? No, he reflected bitterly, none of them could. He'd never made them understand that his own honor had demanded the inquest—that it had been the only way to face Bridlington's father's accusations. No—they would never see that he had been forced into the quarrel; they could not know that the subsequent duels had been fought at the instigation of a vengeful parent. And they did not care, he reminded himself angrily. He'd seen the hatred and felt his aunt's contempt, and he'd been a fool. Aye, what a fool, too, for he'd made a wager to strike back—a stupid, foolish, ridiculous wager. For a tuppence, he'd just forfeit the thousand. Yet in his heart he knew he'd either have to make a push to win or swallow his pride. And it would gall him to have to lose to Charlie.

Rain began to spill soft drops on him and then as the storm gained in intensity he was pelted and soaked thoroughly. Oblivious of the storm, he urged his team on in the darkening afternoon until his anger was spent.

2

Caroline Ashley viewed her charge with a mixture of affection and exasperation. Though only five years Juliana Canfield's senior, it sometimes seemed as though she were expected to fulfill a multitude of roles beyond those she had been employed to do, to wit, to restrain the younger girl's volatility and to guide her through a London Season safely until she could hopefully be turned over to an equally strong-willed husband. Her employment had been a master stroke on the part of her mentor, Miss Richards, headmistress at the select female academy where the very cream of the *ton*'s daughters were instructed in the art of being ladies. That lady, seizing upon the despair of Lady Lenore, had suggested Caroline as a calming influence while informing the Canfields in almost the same breath that Juliana simply could not finish her education there. Sir Maximillian, after hearing the rather daunting list of Juliana's scrapes, had endorsed the proposal almost immediately. Lady Lenore, on the other hand, had demanded to know just how an unmarried female quite on the shelf could expect to guide anyone through a Season when she had not personally experienced one of her own. For once Sir Max had prevailed, and thus had begun an association that Caroline could only consider a mixed blessing—while learning to detest the cold and arrogant Lady Lenore, she had become sincerely attached to Juliana. In a matter of days, she had discovered that it was Lenore Canfield's overbearing, calculating disposition that inspired Juliana to rebellion. Had that lady been less inclined to rule and more inclined to affection, Caro believed the girl would have been better-behaved. But, since nothing short of being a totally insipid beauty would satisfy her mother, Juliana had asserted her independence in more ways than Caro cared to count.

She shuffled through a sheaf of papers sent over by Madame Cecile, the premier modiste to the *ton*, and selected several drawings for the girl's attention. "Take a look at these, my dear, and see what you like," Caroline suggested.

"I don't know. . . . What do you think, Caro?" Juliana mused absently on another matter. "Should I leave a waltz for Ryburn? 'Twill quite fill up my card, and I've no place for Harrington."

"I think," Caroline reproved mildly, "that it is more to the point to examine these sketches so that we may give your mama an answer this morning. Besides, you cannot even know that both gentlemen will ask," she added with a twinkle in her dark eyes. "Really, Ju, but 'tis rather conceited to have your ball card planned even before we reach the Beresfords'."

"Oh, but I know they shall both press me to waltz," Juliana responded airily, "for I am positive that each means to fix his interest to me. Why, Lord Ryburn assures me that I am all the crack, and Lord Harrington writes the most charming poetry to my eyes, as you might remember."

"Charming drivel," Caro observed dryly. "And since you have not the least intention of accepting an offer from either of them, it is not very becoming of you to flirt with them so outrageously." She looked up to see Juliana fluttering her eyelashes over the much-praised cornflower-blue orbs to test the effect in her mirror.

Apparently satisfied, the girl turned back with a giggle. "Oh, Caro, did you *ever* think I should take half so well?" she demanded naively.

"There was never a doubt in my mind, love, although you simply must stop twitting your mama else I shall be turned off." Caroline sobered. "Only this morning, Lady Canfield wished to know how I could have countenanced your dancing three times with young Rupert Rowan at Lady Bennington's. You know full well that to stand up more than twice with the same partner bespeakes a particularity certain to be remarked. And since it is common knowledge that Captain Rowan is nothing but a gazetted fortune hunter, your mama was not amused."

"Oh, Caro, I *am* sorry." The girl was instantly contrite. "Certainly I have not the least interest in Captain Rowan—I swear. He fawns on one in the most excessive way, you know, but I could not help it. I saw Mama watching me like she always does and I did it to vex her. I saw little enough harm at the time." With a sigh, she moved to pick up the sketches that Caroline had selected. "Do not worry about Mama, Caro. She's been in high dudgeon since she came back from West-over. Besides, Papa thinks you quite the most exceptionable companion he could have engaged for me. He says he can see the wonders you have wrought."

"He does not. Juliana, you must give over this tendency to exaggerate."

"But he does—he said so yesterday before you came down to nuncheon—I swear it." She took in Caroline's neat, dark braids, her fine, expressive brown eyes, and her delicately defined profile before confiding further, "You know he said something else, too—that you'd be more than passably pretty if Mama would but spare the blunt to rig you out properly. And he's right—if you had had a Season, you'd be a married lady instead of having to dragon for me."

"A delusion at best," Caroline sighed as Juliana returned to her favorite subject beyond herself. "No, my dear, it would never have happened. Oh, I'll give you that my birth's respectable, but who's to forget that my papa put a period to his own existence rather than go to debtors' jail? And do not be going on about the Gunnings marrying dukes or some such nonsense—that was years and years ago. Now, a man as rich as a nabob desires an heiress."

"Still—"

"Ju, you know 'tis Madame Cecile's busy season. If you would have new gowns, you must decide now." Caroline redirected her charge's attention back to the matter at hand. Pointing to one of the drawings in the younger girl's hand, she persisted, "What do you think of that done up in a soft blue taffeta? Or even in a deeper shade perhaps? And you might consider the other one in a silver gauze, I think."

"Lud, I don't care, Caro—'tis you who have the good taste. I am quite sick of clothes and fittings, if you want the truth of it. 'Tis the only thing Mama seems the least inclined to spend money on, isn't it?"

"Nonetheless, it must be done, my dear. Both your parents are determined to fire you off in style."

"And how do you think I feel, Caro, to go off night after night rigged out in the latest gowns while you trail after in that old rose silk of yours? You have all the instincts as to what is right—yet you cannot even dress above a poor relation! I mean to speak to Papa about it, Caro!"

"You'll do no such thing!" Caroline's dark eyes widened in alarm. "Ju, promise me that you will not! You'll make matters worse for me with your mama if you even attempt it."

"Fiddle."

"You know I was merely engaged to go about with you—Lady Lenore made it quite plain that I was not to put myself forward in the least."

"Well, I do not like it at all. We are friends, are we not, Caro? Oh, I know I was displeased when Mama and Papa hired you, but you were not what I expected. Caro, I like you!"

"Then leave it be!" Caroline burst out with asperity. It was a familiar argument, and one she had no intention of pursuing again. Try as she might, she could never get Juliana to realize the precariousness of her position. The girl refused to understand the jealousy a young female could evoke in a household. "Your pardon for raising my voice, my dear," she sighed. "I fear I am become more like you than the other way around."

"Then perhaps we are good for each other," Juliana responded, "for you will suppress my scrapes and I will give you a modicum of levity. You may have instructed in deportment for Miss Richards, love," she added with a twinkle, "but I suspect you have often wanted to cut up the tiniest dust yourself."

They were interrupted by a tap at the chamber door. Caroline rose to open it to one of the footmen, a fellow with some years' service in the Canfield household. He beamed affectionately across to his master's daughter and lowered his voice almost conspiratorially to announce, "There's a visitor belowstairs for you, Miss Juliana—I took the liberty of putting the person in the blue saloon without disturbing Simpson."

"But who—?"

"Ah . . . one of your cousins, miss."

Both Juliana and Caroline rolled their eyes at the thought of even a few minutes spent with either Miss Charlotte Danvers or Miss Vivian Danvers before Juliana caught the warning in the footman's expression. "Oh." She formed the word silently and nodded. Turning quickly to Caroline, she directed, "Take whichever drawing you like to Mama—I shall be back directly."

"But you'll be at daggers-drawn with your cousin in

minutes, Ju. Perhaps I ought to go down with you to keep the peace."

"No—'twill be all right, I promise. Just tell Mama I will have the silver one, please."

Before Caroline could make sense of her haste, Juliana had slipped down the back stairs with the footman trailing behind her. Fervently hoping that Caroline could detain her mother, she threw open the door with a squeal of delight and ran to hug him.

"Oh, Patrick—'tis you, after all!"

"Hallo. Ju." He grinned as he set her back and disengaged her arms from around his neck. Giving her a quick appraisal, he teased, "Well, I can see that beneath all your fine clothes, there's still an incorrigible hoyden."

"Patrick Danvers, is that any way to greet your favorite cousin?" she demanded in mock pique.

"Given the selection, it ain't much of a distinction, is it?" His hazel eyes lit up in amusement as she tossed her blond curls and moved away to position herself in the best light, making sure that her perfect profile was outlined by the window. "And you can save the flirting for someone who will appreciate it."

"Patrick!"

The amusement faded and he sobered. Abruptly he changed the subject. "You heard what happened at Westover, didn't you?"

"Yes, and it is the most hideously unfair thing! Patrick, 'twas monstrous cruel what Uncle Vernon did."

"Alas, did my aunt not tell you how unfair it was to all of us?"

"But to say you have to marry! And so soon!"

"Oh, I suppose everyone gets leg-shackled eventually, Ju." He smiled at her indignation. "After all, isn't that what you're trying to do with your Season?"

"Well, it's what Mama's trying to do, if that's what you mean." She turned her head to meet his eyes.

"Surely you don't mean to attempt meeting the terms, Patrick—'tis impossible!''

"*Et tu*, Ju?"

"What?"

"You don't have any more faith in my chances than the rest of them, do you? I'd not expected it of you."

"Oh, Patrick—no! 'Tis not that, precisely, but . . . well, can you?"

"I don't know," he answered honestly. "Perhaps. Not that I'll take an Antidote or anything just to get the money. While I'm not as rich as Croesus, I'm comfortable enough that I don't have to sell my name for the family fortune."

"You shouldn't have made the wager, Patrick." Juliana bit her lip as soon as the words had escaped. "Oh, I know—coming from me, that's rich, isn't it? I'd have done the same thing if I'd been facing Charlie and Charlotte, I am sure."

"It was this curst temper of mine," he admitted. "I should've stayed home since I never expected anything from Uncle Vernon anyway. But I will own it was vastly entertaining when old Weatherby read off the rest of the will."

"Mama's still mad as fire."

"So are they all, no doubt." He moved to stand beside her and looked out the unshuttered window for a moment. "Ju, I'll need your help if I am to try pulling this off. I am afraid that the sort of women I know don't qualify under Uncle Vernon's terms." He caught himself and flashed a rueful smile. "Your pardon—I am unused to polite society—I should not have said that."

"Pooh. As if I did not know about barques of frailty and the muslin company, after all. Besides, Patrick, we have always been able to say anything to each other."

"Almost anything," he amended. "Thing is, Ju, I don't know any respectable females."

"No . . ." She shook her head. "If you mean that I

am to present you to eligible ladies, I cannot do it. For one thing, it won't fadge; for another, it would cost Miss Ashley her position with Mama. If it were just me —if I thought it would work—I'd do it, but your suit would not be welcomed, Patrick, and if Mama knew I'd helped you, she'd turn Caro off without a character. She blames Caro for everything, anyway.''

"Caro?"

"My companion. Papa hired her to keep me from getting into scrapes, you know, and I suppose it has worked a little.''

"She's a veritable paragon if it has. The last I heard, you'd been sent home from school for trying to elope with the dancing master.''

" 'Twasn't the dancing master, Patrick—*he* was at least thirty and had the longest nose,'' she remembered mischievously. "If you have to remember the tale, remember it right—'twas the music master—he had soulful eyes and a very fine pair of shoulders, too.''

"Lud, Ju! One could almost pity Aunt Lenore.''

"Patrick . . .'' She sobered suddenly. "If you want the money . . .''

"Well, I'm not in beggars' row, Ju, so it's not so much that,'' he answered, "as the thought of Charlie and Quen and Larry's crowing that prompts me to try.''

She turned away and took a deep breath. "Patrick, there is me.''

He stared, bereft of speech for a moment, at his beautiful cousin. He'd heard she was the Toast of the Season, that Brummell himself had dubbed her "the Canfield Jewel,'' and he knew how determined his aunt was that she make a good match. "No, Ju, I'd not ask you to do it.''

"Patrick—''

"You don't fancy yourself in love with me, do you?'' he asked gently.

"Well, no, but—''

"Then think about what you offer, my dear, before

you throw a brilliant future away. Would you really want to give up your Season to wed with an outcast? That's what I am, after all," he reminded her with a trace of bitterness in his voice.

"I don't care." She spun back around. "Patrick, of all the family, I like you the best—I cannot stand what they have done to you. I'd marry you before I'd let them make a laughingstock of you. Only say that I may bring Caro with me, and—"

"Of everyone I know, Ju, we are the most alike," he interrupted. "No—we should not suit. For one thing, you'd have to change too much—and so would I. You'd flirt, and I'd forever be defending my honor."

"But I wouldn't! I'd be the most unexceptional wife! And I would never have to listen to Mama carp—she'd never speak to me again."

"Well"—he administered the coup de grace—"assuming that everything else worked out, have you considered the degree of intimacy required to obtain a Westover heir?" He watched her eyes widen and nodded his head. "Whether you would like it or not, we'd have to embark immediately to put you into an interesting condition. And assuming we are successful, have you thought that you will be dandling a little redheaded fellow on your knee this time next year? With your coloring and mine, we should most likely produce a carrot-top," he finished with a grin.

"Ugh!"

"Precisely. And think if the poor child should be a girl. We should never fire her off."

"Oh, Patrick!" She began to giggle at the picture of wedded life he painted. "Well, if you insist on describing life with you in those terms, you will not even have to worry about your horrid reputation. There's none to have you."

"Do you think I haven't considered that? How the devil am I to find a female I can tolerate, anyway? And assuming there is such a creature out there, I'm going to have to offer as bold as brass, 'Marry me, miss, and give me an heir so I can be rich.' No doubt I shall be impaled on her hatpin for the suggestion.''

"Well, maybe we can think of something,'' she ventured doubtfully.

The sound of footsteps outside made both of them jump. Juliana moved to rearrange the flowers in a bowl and Patrick turned to study the latticework of the windowpanes. After a soft rap at the door, Caroline Ashley let herself in and moved forward apologetically. Patrick edged around cautiously, took in her dull, drab gray gown, the starched cap atop her braids, and relaxed slightly.

"Your pardon, Juliana, but your mama is looking for you. I promised to fetch you before she came herself. After all—'' She stopped, suddenly aware of the man in the room.

"He is my cousin, Caro—'tis Westover,'' Juliana hastened to explain.

Clearly, the title meant nothing to her and she did not make the connection with the more infamous Patrick Danvers. To keep her at *point non plus*, Patrick moved quickly to bow over her hand while Juliana added, "Westover, may I present my dearest friend, Caroline Ashley? Miss Ashley stays with us for the Season.'' With a wary eye on the open door, she added, "My cousin has but returned to town.''

"I did not mean to intrude, but Lady Canfield was most insistent.''

"Westover was just leaving, Caro. If you will but tell Mama that I shall be up immediately, I'll see him out.''

"Pray do not be long, Ju,'' Caroline urged, "and I will show her the rest of the sketches.''

Patrick watched her leave, much struck by two things —the slight huskiness of her voice and the deep pansy-brown of her eyes. "Is that your dragon, Coz? I'd imagined Aunt Lenore to employ a very different sort of person.''

"Well, you do not know her, of course, but now can you not see why I cannot risk losing her? Lud knows what Mama would find the next time."

"She cannot be very old," he mused slowly.

"She is three-and-twenty, Patrick." Juliana started to follow her companion out, took a few steps, stopped abruptly, and spun around in inspiration. "Patrick, you are quite positive that you do not want to marry me?"

"Ju—"

"Then would you consider Miss Ashley instead? She's the dearest person, really she is, and her situation is quite desperate. Oh, Patrick, Mama keeps her in the direst straits—she has not but three gowns to her name if you do not count that hideous thing she was wearing. And she will not let me go to Papa to get her anything better because she has too much pride. And Mama dislikes her very much. And—"

"Enough! If she took you on, I know she's desperate. There is no need to go to such lengths to convince me of it."

"And she's not given to queer starts like me, I promise, Patrick. She's quite calm, really she is. Her birth's respectable though her father committed suicide when she was but fifteen." When she could see that her cousin was staring at her as if she were queer in the attic, Juliana cast about wildly for the means to convince him. "She's not empty-headed in the least—she's not! She's just like you—reads everything she can find. Indeed, she was such an excellent pupil that Miss Richards kept her on at no fee and even employed her to teach the younger ones. Oh, Patrick, she has nothing! And I should like to see Mama if you should make her Viscountess Westover!"

"Ju—"

"And she cannot have romantical expectations, after all," she pursued naively, "for she considers herself quite on the shelf. Your suit would solve everything for the both of you—it would! All she has to look forward to is the life of a governess once I am fired off.''

"And you think her poor prospects would make me
. . . er, more palatable?''

"Patrick, she's certain to find you attractive. And
though you might not note it, she could be quite pretty
if she had decent gowns and a dresser for her hair.''

"Juliana!'' Lady Canfield called imperiously from
abovestairs.

"Oh, dear—I have to go, Patrick! Mama would be
furious if she even suspected you were here.'' Juliana
rushed to the door and peered anxiously out. "Think on
what I've said—you may see Miss Ashley again at the
Beresfords' this very evening for 'tis Maria's come-out
—and 'twill be such a squeeze that you might manage to
go unremarked.'' With that, she slipped out of the
room.

3

"*Good heavens*!" Lenore Canfield clutched convulsively at her husband's coat sleeve and gaped with astonishment. "Max, 'tis Patrick! How dare he—Max, you must find Juliana ere she is ruined by the assocation—she'll not have sense enough to give him the cut direct. Oh, Max," she moaned, "he'll ruin us."

"Nonsense, Lee," her husband soothed while carefully disengaging her clenched fingers. "He is her cousin, after all, so it is to be expected that they will converse. Besides, I have never thought him half so bad as you would have him. Indeed, I quite like him above any of your other relations."

"How can you say so when you know what he has done to us—after those horrid inquests? Max, you are the most unfeeling of fathers!"

"And I have always believed that we should have brushed through better if the Danvers family had supported Patrick," he reminded her dryly. "He was acquitted—or have you chosen to forget that?"

Ignoring his logic, she continued to fret. "Oh, dear! What can Joanna Beresford be thinking of? And poor Maria! 'Tis her come-out, after all." Lenore craned her neck for a view of their hostess and the honoree, but was denied the satisfaction of seeing their shocked and dismayed expressions since Patrick's tall frame obscured the scene. "Well, there is nothing for it," she decided, "but that we must leave. I would not for the world remind anyone of the connection."

"Lee,"—her husband's voice dropped in warning— "we shall do no such thing. For one thing, I have paid more than a hundred guineas for the gowns you and Juliana are wearing; for another, such a public display of your feelings cannot but dredge up the very scandal you wish to avoid." He smoothed the fabric of his sleeve before carefully placing her hand in the crook of his arm. "Now, we shall go on as planned. You may ignore his presence if you wish, but you will not cause any unpleasantness. That would be far more fatal to your daughter's success than a chance meeting with Patrick," he told her firmly.

But Lady Lenore was not easily mollified, particularly not when she saw the object of her indignation moving from the receiving line to intercept Juliana. "Max," she hissed almost hysterically, "*do something*!"

Unperturbed, Maximillian Canfield forcibly drew his lady away. "Now, Lee," he reminded again, "she is his cousin. And unless I am mistaken, that is Albert Bascombe with him. Ten to one, he is but presenting young Bertie to your daughter."

"Bascombe?" Lenore was temporarily diverted as she digested the possibility. "Is that not the Earl of Haverstoke's heir? I do not believe I have seen him at any of these affairs before."

The transparency of her thoughts amused her husband. "It is—though I should not set my heart on him for a son-in-law, Lee. Bertie Bascombe is certainly no match for Juliana—from all I have heard, the boy's a trifle slow-witted."

"Nonsense," she dismissed, "Haverstoke's got thirty thousand if he's got a farthing, Max. Besides, with Juliana, there's much to be said for an amiable husband."

"Quite the opposite, my dear." Sir Max shook his head. "Our Juliana will require someone quite masterful, I think." He turned to watch his wife's nephew bow over his daughter's hand. "No, she and Patrick are much alike, I am afraid—both quite intelligent, but too headstrong by far. The right match could be the saving grace for each of them, while the wrong one could have disastrous consequences."

At that very moment, Patrick firmly pushed a reluctant Albert Bascombe forward to meet Juliana under the bemused stares of a rather large number of her admirers. The unfortunate Bertie colored uncomfortably and merely goggled speechlessly at the lovely heiress. It was not until Patrick had physically prodded him that the hapless young man found his tongue at all. Ju's blue eyes were full of mischief as they met Patrick's.

"Ah, Coz—so you found your invitation, after all." She smiled.

Bertie, remembering his role finally, managed to stammer out a request to procure some lemonade for her. As if on cue, the gentlemen around them began vying for the favor until Juliana settled the matter by sending each one off in search of a different delectable, leaving her temporarily alone with her cousin in the crowded ballroom.

"Really, Patrick," she observed after Bascombe's retreating form, "but I cannot imagine the association."

"Bertie? Alas, my dear, but I've found friends few enough when I needed them. Bertie at least has that rare quality of constancy in the face of adversity—he has never wavered in his support."

"But he does not appear to have all his wits about him."

"I should characterize him as being a slow thinker rather than half-witted, Ju," Patrick responded.

Out of the corner of her eye, Juliana could see her parents watching her so she moved to the matter at hand. "I collect you had no difficulty getting in?"

"None." He grinned. "If you do not consider my putting Lady Beresford on the verge of the vapors a difficulty. I thought she meant to faint when I kissed her chit's hand."

"Maria? Well, I vow she liked it well enough."

"No—she could not decide whether to flirt or recoil —and, alas, I was gone by the time she'd made up her mind."

"Patrick," Juliana giggled, "you are incorrigible!"

"I? 'Twas not I who came up with this preposterous scheme. By the by . . ." He looked around the room for a moment. "I do not seem to see this charming companion you would foist on me, my dear. If you've dragged me out merely to pique the *ton* for your diversion, Ju, I shall wring your neck."

She considered pouting prettily or rapping him coquettishly with her enameled fan and then thought better of it. For all that could be said of him, he was little given to flirtatious games. Instead, she inclined her head toward a curtained-off area behind the musicians. "I daresay you might find her there, Patrick, for once she's exchanged proper greetings around and seen me establish my crowd, she usually seeks out a place to read. And Mama does not mind because she does not like for Caro to put herself forward, anyway."

"Have you mentioned any of this to her?"

"Caro? Of course not—'twould be most improper of me, don't you think?"

"And when has that ever stopped you?"

"This time I leave it up to you to determine if you will suit, Coz, though I cannot imagine that you would not." Another quick glance at her parents revealed that her mother was still staring at her. "Patrick . . ." She touched his arm impulsively and asked, "Would you waltz with me?"

With raised eyebrow, he reached for the card that dangled from her wrist. "Really, my dear, but there's no room—'twould seem I am too late for the honor."

"Pooh. You are Patrick Danvers, after all, so who's to quibble? Besides, you are quite the handsomest man in this room."

"I'd ruin you," he reminded her bluntly. "No—despite what you both seem to think, I was not born to vex Aunt Lenore."

Before she could wheedle and coax, he executed a quick little bow and turned his attention to the alcove behind the musicians. It seemed to him that he could literally hear his aunt sigh with relief as he moved away.

Safely hidden by the curtains, Caroline shifted her position in one of the straight-backed chairs to gain more illumination from the candle sconce above her. Unconsciously she slid a kid slipper off her foot and settled back to read again. Bending her head low to see the page, she failed to note that she was no longer alone.

"Do you mind if I join you, Miss Ashley?"

She jumped guiltily and looked up to take in the tall frame and handsome face of Juliana's cousin. "Since I have but one book, I fail to see how 'tis possible, sir," she responded waspishly to his intrusion. The smile faded from his eyes and she was instantly contrite. "Your pardon, sir—I did not mean you were unwelcome," she managed as she searched for her shoe with her stockinged foot.

"Allow me."

Before she could fathom his intent, he had dropped to one knee and retrieved the slipper, slid it on, and tied the narrow strap at her ankle. Red-faced, she tried to draw her foot away, but he held it firmly. When he looked up, there was a hint of amusement in the hazel eyes that temporarily nonplussed her.

"Thank you, sir—but would you mind unhanding my foot?" Then, suddenly realizing how high-handed she must sound, she managed a self-conscious little smile. To her relief, he released her ankle and took the chair next to hers.

"So, Miss Ashley, what is so fascinating that it tempts you away from the squeeze out there?" he asked as he reached to close the open book over her fingers and read aloud, "*Pride and Prejudice*, eh? I quite like Miss Austen's works myself, although I prefer *Sense and Sensibility* over this one." He flipped the cover back open and noted the dog-eared condition of the novel. "Not the first time through this one, I'd have to say," he observed.

"Nor the second," she admitted ruefully. "I find books I enjoy are like friends—they bear a continuing acquaintance as one discovers something new about them each time they are met." She raised her dark eyes to meet his. "Silly of me, isn't it?"

"Not at all. While I am fond of Austen's works, I cannot say I've read any of them twice. Shakespeare, on the other hand, is quite another matter. And I'm afraid my copy of his sonnets is positively falling to pieces."

"You are funning with me, sir," she accused stiffly.

"I assure you I am not. Indeed, I'll bring it with me the next time we meet and you can see for yourself," he promised solemnly despite a twinkle that lit his eyes.

"My lord . . . Westover, is it? Gentlemen of the *ton* do not usually admit to reading anything other than the *Gazette*."

"Ah, but then I am lately come into my title, so I daresay I've not learned all the finer points of being a viscount."

"Now I know you are funning with me."

"No." The twinkle faded as he admitted, "I've not gone about much and certainly I've not spent any time surveying the Marriage Mart. It all seems a foolish and empty pastime, if you want my opinion."

"It *is* a foolish and empty pastime," she agreed readily. "But 'tis a ritual to be followed nonetheless if one is to be successful socially. To even admit to being different, unless one becomes the latest fashionable rage as Brummell has done, is social suicide. Somehow, sir, I cannot think a passion for Shakespeare will make you fashionable. Now, if it were Byron—''

"Oh, I quite like him, too . . . and Shelley and Scott and young Keats . . . Coleridge, Wordsworth, Lamb—I like all of them except perhaps Rogers, who is too acerbic for me. But actually I prefer the classics even more—Homer, Virgil, Ovid, Tacitus' histories. In short, Miss Ashley, if it is printed, I am not above reading it.''

She stared at him in fascination, uncertain whether to believe him. Finally a smile quirked at the corners of her mouth. "Somehow, sir, I cannot think a passion for literature will make you fashionable. When you are amongst the *ton*, you must affect an ennui, you must give far more attention to your shirt points and your cravats than your mind, and you must appear totally absorbed in the pursuits of your own pleasure.''

"The advice of a seasoned dragon, eh?"

"No—merely an observation.''

"Tell me, Miss Ashley—how is it that you come to be in Lady Canfield's employ? You seem rather young for the task of companioning my hoyden cousin through her first Season.''

She set aside her book and folded her hands in her lap while she considered how best to answer him. It was, after all, an impertinent question, and one that she need not even try to answer. But then, he seemed unaware of the impertinence and there was something about him that she instinctively liked. Certainly there was nothing condescending or patronizing in his manner. Finally she nodded. "I am three-and-twenty, sir, and quite on the shelf myself, but I have taught deportment at Miss Richards' Select Academy for Young Ladies since I was eighteen. When Juliana . . .'' She hesitated, wondering how much of the story he'd heard. "When Juliana left the academy, Miss Richards recommended me to Lady Canfield, saying that Juliana would be far more likely to listen to me than to an elderly chaperon.''

"An unenviable task, I should think."

"Oh, no! I quite like Juliana, you see, and I do think that I must have some influence."

"If she has gone a month without getting into a scrape, I'd say you were worth a fortune to Aunt Lenore."

"Would that I were, but alas, I am not."

He took in her faded gown, its alterations evident even in the faint light of the candles, and felt a stirring of sympathy for her. Juliana had been right. Caroline Ashley was not an ill-looking girl—quite pleasing, in fact—intelligent, sensible, and possessed of a sense of humor. While definitely taller than the fashion, she held herself proudly and showed a trim, well-defined figure. That her hair was dark in a time when blonds were the fashion did not bother him at all. There was something about her that bespoke quality without affectation. On impulse, he leaned over to examine her bookmark and found it to be her dance card. It was empty.

"I see you have saved a waltz for me," he told her lightly.

"No—I do not dance this evening, sir."

"But you can waltz, can you not?"

"I have practiced some," she admitted.

"How fortunate for us both." He flashed his most engaging smile and penned his name next to one of the numbers. "Let us hope I have hit it aright, Miss Ashley, for I despise rondels."

Her eyes widened at his easy, open manner. It was inconceivable enough that this handsome, well-favored man would seek her out to speak with her, but to single her out to waltz—well, he must be misadvised as to her situation. And before he embarked on a flirtation that could only be painful for her, she felt the need to explain, "My lord, I think it incumbent on me to point out that my card is empty because I am totally ineligible. I—"

"I know." He grinned. "You are on the shelf."

"No . . . yes . . ." She twisted her hands against the silk skirt. "That is to say—well, I have no expectations, sir."

"Since I have but recently had any myself, I'd scarce consider that an ineligibility," he told her in his best sober voice.

"I'm afraid I've understated the case then. I have absolutely none—not a farthing above what Lady Canfield pays me."

"Then you are in the basket." He nodded. "But I fail to see—"

"Lord Westover, if I go out there and dance with you, 'twill be remarked and 'twill be said that I am casting out lures to you, when—"

"When 'tis I who am casting out lures to you," he finished for her.

"No! I did not mean it like that, I assure you."

"But the tabbies can be cruel. I understand, my dear, but I'm undeterred by your poverty or by the gossips, so . . . shall we waltz, Miss Ashley?"

"You do not understand! 'Tis worse than that even." She took a deep breath and sighed. "There's no way to wrap it up in clean linen, sir. My father gamed away his inheritance, my mother's portion, and my expectations. Then, when I was ready to leave school, he could not face debtors' jail." She dropped her eyes and lowered her voice. "He put a period to his existence and cheated everyone."

"Juliana already told me that."

"But—"

"How very poorly you must think of me, Miss Ashley, if you would believe I'd hold your father's shortcomings against you. After all," he added in bald understatement, "I am scarce above reproach myself." He reached to possess her hand and she was suddenly conscious of strength and reassurance in his grip. "Come," he coaxed, "I'd truly like to dance with you."

"Well," she relented under the warmth of his gaze,

"I suppose there's little enough harm if we make it plain that I've no intention of setting my cap for you."

"Done."

She allowed him to lead her out as the first few bars of a waltz began. It seemed as though the crowd parted to make room for them until she found herself clasped lightly in his arms. At first, she was acutely conscious of the stares around her and then the music took over and she no longer had to count out her steps in her mind. His hand was warm on hers and the fresh clean scent of the Hungary water he'd used for shaving wafted between them. There was a strong masculinity about the arm that encircled her waist and held her to him. Uncharacteristically, she found herself wanting to lean on him, to rest her head on his broad shoulder. When she looked up, she found him studying her with those strange, beautiful eyes. And then the dream crashed down into reality.

"You know, Miss Ashley," he murmured above her ear, "you deserve better than you have. A female like you ought to have pretty things—fancy dresses, jewels, pin money . . ."

"Oh?" She stiffened slightly and tried to prepare herself for what was coming.

He failed to note the edge that had crept into her voice as he plunged ahead. "I mean, just think on it— look at this gown you are wearing . . ."

Her color heightened ominously as she managed through clenched teeth, "Really? And what, pray tell, is wrong with my gown?"

"Well, I'm scarce an authority on female apparel, Miss Ashley, but even I can tell you have altered it several times. Once it had a much fuller skirt, as was the fashion some twenty years ago. Then there is the waist —I can see that it has been raised in the French fashion. And you've removed a flounce to make sleeves—"

"I am well aware of what I've done to it," she gritted out.

"But 'tis unnecessary economy, Miss Ashley. If you would but listen to what I would say—"

"And I suppose you are wishful of giving me these things I have been lacking?" she ventured with sudden deceptive sweetness.

"As a matter of fact, I am," he admitted.

To his utter surprise, she pushed him away angrily and stalked off, leaving him to stand like the veriest fool amid the whirling figures of the other dancers. Mercifully, the music ended swiftly. Threading his way across the floor after her, he caught up. "You did not hear me out," he told her as he spun her around by the shoulder.

"I didn't have to, Lord Westover," she answered coldly, "for while I may be poor, I am not so sunk in depravity that . . . that . . . Oh, how *dare* you think such a thing!" Shaking off his hand, she plunged headlong into the crowd.

"What the devil are you talking about?" he called after her. "Wait!"

"I say, Patrick—is that your Miss Ashley?" Bertie Bascombe stepped in front of him. "Passably pretty girl, but I think m'mother had a dress something like that when I was in short coats. You'll have to—"

"Oh, there you are, Patrick." Juliana pushed past Bertie to confront her cousin. "Whatever can you have been thinking of?" she demanded. "Mama saw you with Caro out on the floor and she's mad as fire. I hope Caro's accepted you, because I don't think I can help her now. And Papa's going to York tomorrow, so he won't be able to do anything either."

By then Patrick realized that Caroline Ashley was nowhere to be seen. Frustrated, he snapped, "Cut line, Ju! I tried to make friends with the girl, but you didn't tell me she was given to queer starts! I'd have done better if I'd tried to abduct her!"

"Caro? Patrick, whatever can you have said to her?" Juliana wanted to know. "She's the most even-tempered creature I know. But Mama—"

"Hang Aunt Lenore! Ju, don't go acting me a Cheltenham tragedy just because I danced with your Miss Ashley. If my aunt was watching so closely, she'd know I was left standing on the floor. Females! All I said to the girl was that she needed some pretty clothes and things, I swear." He caught Juliana's stunned look and suddenly it came home to him what he'd done. "Oh, lud!" he groaned. "I made a mull of it, Ju."

"Pat, let's leave," Bertie insisted, " 'cause I see your Aunt Lenore coming this way and it don't bode well for Miss Canfield, I can tell."

"No, I've got to try to find Miss Ashley . . . got to explain—"

"Patrick, I'll try to talk to her," Juliana offered quickly. "Mr. Bascombe's right—you'd best go. I'll send you a note round in the morning, I promise."

4

"Tell me, Caro, what did you really think of him?" Juliana asked casually over her morning chocolate.

"Who?"

"Oh, you know very well who! Patrick!"

"I'm surprised you can ask after that scene with your mama last night," Caroline responded dryly. "Really, Ju, but it was poor of you not to have warned me that Westover and Patrick Danvers are one and the same. My credit has been quite destroyed, my reputation probably damaged beyond repair, and my employment nearly ended—and you would know what I think of him?"

"But did you not think him quite the handsomest man you have ever seen?" Juliana pursued slyly. "I mean, did you not like him?"

"Oh, it was a very near thing, I admit it, and I was almost deceived into thinking him kind even, but then I discovered what he was about. And that was before your mama read that peal over me. Had it not been for your father, I should have been turned off without character in the middle of the night. No, Ju—what you and your cousin did was not handsome at all."

"Still, he did single you out to waltz."

"Most probably because I was the only female green enough to go," Caroline noted severely. "Had I had a father or brother to protect me—or someone to warn me even—he'd not have been so bold. Devil Danvers they call him! Ju, how could you have let me be so foolish?"

"Patrick's not what you hear of him, Caro—I promise he is not. He's good and kind and honorable—I know he is."

"Then you are besotted! Cousin or no, you would forget he's a rake and a murderer and a gamester! And he had the effrontery to offer me carte blanche!"

"But you mistook the matter, Caro. He—"

"I assure you that I did not. I know I should not be speaking to you of such things, Ju, but he did. Now, if you are wishful of my company, you will not speak of him again to me."

"Poor Caro," Juliana sympathized. "Mama can be such a trial when she wants to be, I know, but you should not let her poison your mind against Patrick before you get to know him."

"I have no intention of getting to know him. Indeed, I—"

"Miss Ashley?" Juliana's maid stuck her head around a silken screen. "Thomas said I was to tell you that you have a caller in the library, miss."

"There must be a mistake. Lady Canfield does not allow—"

"No mistakin' the matter, miss—Thomas said I was to tell you."

"But who . . . ?"

"As to that, Thomas didn't say. He just told me that it was about a book."

"A book? Caro, you haven't ordered another book, have you?" Juliana demanded. "You know 'tis folly to buy more when you need so many other things. Besides, we can borrow on our subscription to Hookham's Lending Library."

"No," Caroline mused thoughtfully, "I have ordered nothing. Besides, the delivery of a book would not require a morning call. Well, I daresay I shall just have to find out for myself," she decided. "I doubt I shall be gone above a trice, my dear, but you'd best be getting ready for your fitting at Madame Cecile's while I am belowstairs."

Her curiosity whetted, Caro went down. It was inconceivable that anyone should be calling on her, particularly since Lady Canfield had judiciously put it about that her daughter's companion was a distant poor relation with no expectations. That, coupled with her scanty wardrobe, had assured that Caro Ashley would attract no more than a passing glance of sympathy from anyone.

She paused to smooth the skirt of her favorite dress, a blue muslin given her by Miss Richards, before opening the door to Sir Max's library. The room was quite dim, made so by a combination of dark wood, closed draperies, and the overall dreariness of a rainy day. Thomas, the footman, pulled the heavy window hangings open before making a discreet exit. In a corner, Caroline's visitor appeared absorbed in a study of Maximillian Canfield's bookshelves. For a moment, Caro thought her eyes were deceiving her as they traveled over his tall frame to the unmistakable deep rich red of his hair. For a fleeting moment she was torn between the impulse to run and a desire to deliver a stinging rebuke. Apparently her thoughts were mirrored on her face, for when he turned around, his first words were, "Don't go—please." Then, with a rueful smile, he extended a well-worn book toward her. "My copy of the sonnets—'tis in sadder condition than your *Pride and Prejudice*, I fear."

"You!" she choked.

"Alas, yes. Miss Ashley, I've come to offer my apologies for the misunderstanding last night. I collect that—"

"Lord Westover"—she rounded on him—"if Lady Canfield had the slightest notion that you were here to call on me, I should be discharged on the instant. As it is, I have endured not only the insult you offered me but also the worst reading of my character in my entire life! Now, if you will excuse me—"

"No. I have something to say that might improve your situation."

"At the risk of plain speaking, sir, if you do not leave before Lady Lenore finds you are here, I will not have a situation."

"Miss Ashley, you mistook my meaning last night," Patrick tried to explain as he moved closer. " 'Twas not my intent to offend you, I assure you."

"Please—just leave."

"Do you think I cannot tell a devilish straitlaced female when I see one?" he asked.

"And I do not care what you can tell, my lord. I think it outside of enough that neither you nor Juliana felt it necessary to tell me just who you were before I'd made a fool of myself in front of my employer and half the *ton.* Now Lady Lenore tells me my reputation is quite ruined and I am unfit to accompany Juliana publicly." Her eyes flashed indignantly as she bit off each word. "In short, for whatever amusement it has afforded you, you have nigh ruined me." Her piece said, she turned to go.

"That being the case, Miss Ashley," he answered as he stepped in front of her to block her path, "I must ask you to hear me out. 'Twas my intention to make you an honorable offer of marriage." Speechless, she could only stare while he hastened to explain, "I find myself in need of a wife, Miss Ashley, and I think you meet my requirements."

"Your requirements," Caroline echoed faintly. "And what, pray, are they?"

"Well, you do not appear to suffer from an excess of sensibility, you seem to be an intelligent female, and your situation here cannot be a pleasant one." He paused while she digested his words, and then he added gently, "I think I can offer you a better life than you have here, Miss Ashley. Wed with me and you will have pretty gowns, jewelry, a home to manage—the things a female wants."

"You jest, of course."

"I assure you I do not, Miss Ashley. I have one week less than a year in which to marry and produce an heir." His hazel eyes were sober as they met hers. "I can make you a very rich woman."

"No."

"I pray you will consider before you answer," he pressed her. "You would not find me an uncomfortable husband, my dear."

"This must be a jest—you cannot possibly want to marry me—you do not even know me."

"Of course I don't want to marry you—I don't want to marry anyone, to be perfectly candid. But I am reconciled to the necessity of it, and I'm not repining, Miss Ashley. You've a trim enough figure, and with the help of a good modiste and a dresser, you'll be a credit to me, I am sure. And—your pardon for plain speaking, my dear—once the heir is assured, you'll not find me a demanding husband."

"You *are* serious," she decided finally.

He nodded. "I knew you were a reasonable female from the first. I suggest you say nothing to anyone other than Juliana until you are removed from this house. Aunt Lenore can make one deuced uncomfortable when she wants to, and there's no need for you to endure her tongue. I'll return with a special license this afternoon, and we can be at Westover by nightfall." Reaching to lift her chin with his hand, he bent closer until his face was only a few inches from hers. "I believe 'tis customary to seal the bargain with a kiss, Miss Ashley."

"Bargain?" Her color heightened dangerously and she jerked away. "Of all the conceited . . . the arrogant . . the audacious things I have ever heard in my life! I take leave to tell you, sir, that I decline what I can only deem a preposterous offer!''

"You are being hasty, Miss Ashley. You've not considered—"

"Hasty! *Hasty*?" she flashed indignantly. "You've barely met me, and—"

Stung, he snapped, "And I've made you an honorable offer of marriage, Miss Ashley! I regret that it seems precipitate, but I've not the time or the inclination for a lengthy courtship. I thought, given your circumstances and everything, that you would be grateful to—"

"You thought . . . you thought that I should be grateful to ally myself with . . . with a hardened gamester, a . . . a . . ."

"Murderer?" he supplied grimly. "No, I thought you sensible enough to recognize the advantages of the match, if you want the truth. After all, you can scarce expect me to dangle after you. It's not like you are likely to receive another offer, but if you—"

"No. I have not the least intention of selling my person for dresses and pin money—and so I shall tell Juliana when I go upstairs. Again, if you will excuse me . . ." Finding him in her way, she collected herself enough to order, "Pray step aside, sir."

Patrick was unprepared for the rush of emotion he felt as he took in her flushed cheeks and the fire in her dark eyes. The girl had spirit and it showed from the straightness of her carriage to the jut of her chin. His own eyes warmed as they traveled over her. "You would not find it an unpleasant experience, I think," he murmured.

To her utter horror, he grasped her shoulders, and before she realized his intent, he bent his head to hers. Her eyes widened and then shut tightly as he kissed her thoroughly. It was her first real kiss, and it send oddly disjointed thoughts through her mind. She was acutely aware of the softness of his breath against her face, the feel of his lips on hers, and the strength of his arms as they enveloped her. Resolutely she stiffened and pushed him away.

He released her abruptly and stepped back. "Your pardon, Miss Ashley—I shouldn't have done that." He watched her touch her lips with her fingers. The color had drained from her face.

"I should think it all of a piece," she choked when she found her voice finally. " 'Tis expected of Devil Danvers!" Brushing past him, she did not pause until she reached the door. "Good day, Lord Westover," she muttered through clenched teeth before she disappeared into the hall.

He started to go after her and then thought better of it—he knew nothing he could say would redeem her opinion of him. With a sigh, he tucked his dog-eared volume of Shakespeare into his coat and left. Outside, Albert Bascombe waited for him.

"I say . . ." Bertie goggled as Patrick swung into the carriage seat across from him. One look at his friend's set face was enough—while Bertie's powers of perception were not the best, they were adequate to warn him against saying anything further. Instead, he leaned back and waited helplessly.

"I've made a mull of it!" Patrick exploded finally. "I behaved like a damned fool, Bertie! I had no more address than a callow youth!"

"Didn't look like your sort of female anyway," Bertie consoled. "Tell you what—we'll look around for another one. I heard Witherspoon's got five of 'em to fire off—and he's not got a feather to fly with. Ten to one, you can buy one of 'em, Patrick."

"No—I was a damned fool to think I could do it."

"Pat—"

"Do you know what she called me? Devil Danvers! Bertie, it's been three years and I've not lived it down yet! If a penniless female at my aunt's mercy cannot be brought to see any advantage to me, I'm at *point non plus*!"

"You sound like you wanted the chit."

"I could have tolerated her. She at least reads something besides the latest Crim Cons. And she can talk without simpering."

"Well, there's m'sister Gussie," Bertie mused. "Thing is, m'father'd cut up a devil of a dust and—"

"Bertie, your sister Augusta's not out of the schoolroom, and if I remember correctly, she doesn't talk."

"Well, she reads," Bertie defended.

"No, there's no help for it—I mean to forfeit."

"Pat, you've got a year," Bertie argued. "Tell you what—we'll put our heads together and come up with a respectable girl for you."

"Thank you, but I am not so thick-skinned that I relish letting another female call me Devil Danvers whilst she rejects my suit," Patrick responded dryly. "Much as I hate to do it, when I get back from Newmarket, I'm going to find Charlie and pay. It isn't as if I wanted a wife, anyway."

5

Alarmed by Patrick's admission that he intended to forfeit the wager with Charles Danvers, Albert Bascombe decided to take matters into his own hands. After all, had not Patrick come to his aid more than once? And did he not deserve better than the certain ridicule of his own family? With those questions firmly answered in his mind, Bertie bent his rather convoluted thought processes to the task of solving his friend's problem.

It stood to reason that if Patrick had offered for Miss Ashley, she must have been an unexceptional girl. And certainly Patrick's refusal to put it to the touch again with another eligible female made Bertie think that it would have to be Caroline Ashley. Once he had arrived, after laborious deliberations at that conclusion, Bertie made up his mind to pay Patrick back for a host of kindnesses by delivering the girl. Finally, with the help of a bottle of his father's best Madeira, he brooded over the matter until he figured out just how to do it.

Feigning business in London, Bertie begged off from accompanying Patrick to Newmarket for the races, and then took the three days of his friend's absence to put his preposterous scheme to work. It had been a difficult task at best for Bertie, who had shied away from females ever since Patrick had rescued him from the clutches of a very mercenary bit of fluff, but he'd screwed his courage to the sticking point and made the acquaintance of Miss Ashley. And in the course of a very stilted morning call, he'd managed to find out that she had more than a passing interest in horses, a circumstance that fit his plans perfectly. From there, it was possible to invite her to drive out in Hyde Park behind the bang-up-to-the-mark grays that Patrick had helped him find at Tattersall's. She'd almost declined, but Miss Canfield persuaded her to go. Bertie had to congratulate himself on how well he'd done.

Now he labored over the two notes he planned to leave for Patrick and the Canfields. Worse than an indifferent scholar, he scratched out two very different explanations, pausing from time to time to make corrections in his abysmal spelling by writing another choice above the first. Then, finding he'd left out something he'd wanted to say, he added lines in the margins until he had to turn the pages around to read what he'd written. Finally satisfied that he'd covered everything, he sanded each letter to dry the blots he'd made and then sealed them before directing his butler as to their delivery.

That done, he ordered the packing of his portmanteau while he dressed with infinite care. After ruining no fewer than six neckcloths, he finally gave in to the ministrations of his valet. It seemed that he was never destined to achieve even the simplest tasks with the ease of someone like Patrick, who, as far as Bertie could tell, excelled in everything. Well, this time, it would be Bertie Bascombe who did Patrick Danvers a good turn—it would be Patrick thanking Bertie for a change. With that comforting thought, he threw back his shoulders and prepared for the adventure of his life.

By the time he presented himself at the Canfield house, he was about to lose his nerve. Only the consolation that he was helping Patrick secure a fortune spurred him to lift the knocker on the great double doors of Sir Max's house.

Above him, Juliana Canfield peered out the window and giggled. "Caro, come look—'tis your gentleman caller."

Flashing the younger girl a look that plainly said her patience was sorely tried, Caroline Ashley lifted another curtain to look down. "Your mama is not going to like this, Ju. And he is not my gentleman caller," she added severely. "Of all the cork-brained things you have gotten me into, this must surely be the worst. I could have cheerfully wrung your neck when you all but accepted for me. Ju, I shall be amazed if Albert Bascombe can maintain a conversation above five minutes."

"Nonsense. He was here at least fifteen."

"And you did most of the speaking."

"I know, but he is *so* rich," Juliana drew out in a perfect imitation of Lady Lenore. "I mean, what is conversation when there is a fortune to be had?"

"Stop it! I daresay that young Bascombe means to court you, but has not the wits about him to do it. No doubt I shall be treated to a plea for help," Caro muttered dryly.

"No." Juliana was positive. "I think he means to fix his interest with you—and Mama will be mad as fire."

"That's why you did this to me, you wretch, isn't it? To pique your mama even if I have to endure an afternoon of trying to follow Bascombe's rather disjointed attempts to speak. I vow that the next time that Conniston calls on you, I shall tell him you've set your mind on seeing the ruins at Wells."

"Caro, you'd do no such thing! He's forty if he's a day—and Mama positively toadeats him just because he's supposed to have thirty thousand in the 'Change."

Caro sighed as a tap sounded at the door. "I suppose there's no help for it this time, but I warn you, Ju—if you ever do this to me again, I shall go back to Miss Richards.''

"But, Caro"—Juliana grinned mischievously—"you must think of the advantages. If Bertie Bascombe does come up to scratch, you just might be a countess someday. Then you may outrank Mama, for Papa is but a baronet, while Bertie's father is an earl."

"Thank you, but I do not aspire to the distinction." With that, Caro gathered up her rather worn bottle-green pelisse and drew it on over her brown walking dress. "I know—I should wait to put this on, but I've no wish for the assistance. I daresay I shall be back shortly, for I expect Bascombe's conversation to be exhausted ere we get to the corner."

"Fiddle. I'll warrant you have a positively exciting time, Caro—if you cannot like him, you will at least get to be seen in Hyde Park. Who knows—if it becomes common knowledge that Albert Bascombe's calling, perhaps 'twill bring others."

"With my expectations?" Caroline lifted a disbelieving eyebrow. "My dear, the next time we go to Hookham's, I mean to have a look at those romances you are borrowing."

"Never forget that you could have been my cousin's viscountess, Caro," Juliana reminded her.

"Much good that would have done me, my dear," Caroline murmured as she pulled on a serviceable pair of brown kid gloves. "I should have been left in the country to increase alone whilst your cousin continued his gaming and dueling. Thank you, but I can think of a hundred things I should rather do."

Picking up her chip-straw hat, she settled it over the dark coil of her braids and deftly tied the ribbon under her chin. "There—that should about do it, don't you think?"

"Caro, can you not be romantical in the least?"

"Not in the least. Females in my circumstances cannot afford to cherish foolish dreams, my dear."

"Caro—"

"Do not be worrying over me. I'll come about—and without setting my cap for a fat purse."

When Caroline reached the landing, she could see Albert Bascombe pacing the marble-tiled entryway like a trapped animal. He looked up just as she negotiated the last few steps and his pale eyes brightened with approval.

"I say, Miss Ashley, but you are deuced prompt for a female," he commended. "M'sisters say they are ready and then leave me standing an hour." Taking in her hat and pelisse, he nodded. "And when you get down, you are ready to leave—I like that."

"Thank you."

He seemed to hesitate for a moment, then threw back his somewhat frail shoulders much in the manner of a servant assuming a burden. "Well, then I daresay we'd best be going."

To Caroline's surprise, the waiting conveyance was a traveling coach complete with liveried driver and coachmen. She hesitated. It was one thing to take a turn in a public park in a barouche or a landaulet or a phaeton, but to be alone with a gentleman in a closed carriage was something else. For a fleeting moment she thought about going back for Juliana or one of the maids, but then after another look at the pale, freckle-faced young man at her side, she decided that he was obviously quite harmless. Besides, it was unlikely that she would be recognized by anyone outside the coach.

"Ain't a whip like Patrick," Bertie responded to her questioning look. "Can't drive—never could. Besides, curricle's got a broken axle."

"Patrick?"

"Westover. He can drive to an inch."

"I see. Tell me, Mr. Bascombe, are you a particular friend of Lord Westover's."

"Uh . . . know him, that's all. Just meant he can drive, but I can't."

"Oh."

As he was handing her up, Bertie almost lost his balance and Caro had to steady herself by clasping the doorjamb. "Your pardon," he mumbled, "but I ain't used to females. Got no address, either."

"But you have sisters," Caroline reminded him.

"Don't take 'em anywhere, if I can help it."

"But you talk to them, don't you?"

"Sometimes. Thing is, Gussie's still in the school-room and Georgie's married. Not that I liked Georgie anyway, mind you, 'cause I didn't. Got tired of her sayin' I was a slowtop." He paused to consider. "But Fanny's all right—don't know I'm a slowtop yet." He bumped his head and fell into the seat across from her. "Oh," he groaned, "I did it again. Patrick said—" He caught himself guiltily and shook his head. "Heard Westover say once," he amended, "that one of them head-measuring fellows would have a devil of a time with mine."

"A phrenologist?"

"That what they call 'em? Uh-huh—guess he would, 'cause I've always got bumps all over. Daresay it's all a hum anyway, you know. You ever get your head measured?'

"No. I think it's a hum too," she answered with a smile.

"You do?" He brightened, grateful to have some-thing to talk about. "Well, when we was in our cups, Patrick let some fellow look at his, and y'know what? Fellow was a dashed loose screw! Said Patrick's amatory instincts needed checking, if you can believe it! Like he was some sort of rakehell or something!"

"Uh—"

"Oh. Shouldn't be talking about such things to a female, I guess. Well," he changed the subject abruptly, "do you speak any French?"

"Yes."

"Good, 'cause I don't and one of us ought to."

"I beg your pardon?"

"I mean, it's an accomplishment."

"I suppose it is. At Miss Richards, every young lady must be fluent ere she is finished."

"I couldn't learn it," he admitted simply.

"I suspect you are too critical of yourself, sir. And even if you did not master French, there must be any number of things in which you excel."

"You think so?" he asked doubtfully. "I must say I ain't found 'em yet. Now, Patrick—he's the downy one —he's got the brains and the looks."

"Then he does not use them—the brains, I mean," she retorted acidly. "And if you do not mind, I would very much rather not discuss someone I've taken into dislike."

"But you have it all wrong, Miss Ashley. Patrick ain't like anyone thinks—he ain't." His face earnest, Bertie leaned across the seat toward Caroline. "Everybody thinks he's a bad fellow, but they don't know it was Bridlington that caused it. Came out at the inquest—his papa tried to quash the evidence. Patrick was acquitted, Miss Ashley. And if that ain't enough, Bridlington's papa encouraged Standen and Haworth to quarrel with Patrick, 'cause he thought they could take him if the weapon was a sword. After the Standen affair, I tried to get Patrick to go abroad, but he couldn't see that he ought to—said he'd fought a fair duel and he'd be *hanged* if he ran. I told him that what with Bridlington's papa so hot for his blood, he'd deuced well be hanged if he stayed. But it ain't like Patrick to run, Miss Ashley— it ain't. And he was acquitted again. Then with Haworth, they did not even have an inquest. Thing is, with a rich man like Bridlington trying to ruin him, don't see how Patrick can come about. 'Course, he ain't tried," Bertie admitted with a sigh as he leaned back against the squabs again. "He ain't received, but he don't try to be, either. Look at Rotherfield—he was just like Patrick, but he still goes everywhere. Oh, there's them that cuts him, but then there's them that doesn't.''

"I was not referring to Lord Westover's past difficulties, Mr. Bascombe,'' Caroline cut in, "but rather to his arrogance.''

"Arrogance?'' Bertie took indignant exception. "Patrick ain't arrogant, Miss Ashley! He's the deuced decent! And there ain't anyone more honorable than Patrick Danvers—I don't care who you would say—there ain't! You know something, Miss Ashley? I'm a slowtop—always was—and when we was boys, the other fellows laughed at me, but not Patrick. I can tell you that if he hadn't been my friend, I'd have been in the basket more times than I can count. Why, he rescued me from the gaming hells before m'father disowned me, he got me out of the clutches of the cent per cents with his own money, and when I got in trouble with the muslin company, he got me out of that too. Come to find out, the baggage was trying to get me to pay for Crofton's brat! And he fought Haworth over me, too—that's how Bridlington planned to get him. When Patrick wouldn't fight, Haworth turned on me and called me out. Patrick knew I'd be carved like a duck, so he met a man that everyone thought would kill him. And you know what? 'Twas Haworth that died from the wound when it turned putrid. And it could have been me.''

"Your loyalty to Lord Westover is commendable,'' Caroline soothed when Bertie stopped to catch his breath. "Unfortunately, his family does not share your opinion of him. And I've no wish to—''

"Because he embarrassed 'em!'' Bertie snorted. "They wanted him to run—to stay away until people forgot. Oh, aye, the Danverses would have liked him better, but Bridlington was calling him a murderer. So he let 'em arrest him, and it was a very near thing, I can tell you. If it hadn't been proved that Bridlington paid to have his son's weapon hidden, Patrick would have swung on the Nubbin' Cheat!''

"Mr. Bascombe, 'twas not my intent to distress

you," Caroline tried again. "Perhaps if we talked about something else, it would be better."

"Your pardon, Miss Ashley—shouldn't have run on like that, I suppose, but I get tired of hearing about what a rounder Patrick is."

"Well, your defense of your friend is commendable, I am sure."

Having said his piece, Bertie found himself at a loss for further conversation. In less than five minutes, he'd said more to a female than he'd said in five years and now he had nothing left to say. He turned to stare out the carriage window into the London street. When Caroline found it necessary to comment on the various landmarks, Bertie responded in monosyllables until she abandoned the attempt. They sat in strained silence for perhaps another fifteen minutes until she suddenly noted their direction.

"Mr. Bascombe, we cannot reach the park this way. Perhaps you should stop and direct your driver before we are hopelessly lost."

He'd hoped she wouldn't discover his plan quite so soon, but for a female, she was deuced clever. Bertie drew in a deep breath before turning back to look at her. "Can't," he told her at last.

"I beg your pardon?"

"Can't," he repeated. "We ain't going for a turn in the park, Miss Ashley. Deuced sorry for it, but I am abducting you."

"You jest," she decided matter-of-factly.

"No."

"Mr. Bascombe, this is ridiculous. Why would you wish to abduct me?"

"Mean to marry you. Knew you would not entertain my suit if I asked." He repeated the carefully memorized lines he'd practiced. When she stared at him, he looked at the floor and mumbled, "Knew you wouldn't. Slowtop," he added succinctly, as though that explained everything.

"But you do not even know me."

"Knew that if Patrick thought you was all right, you must be."

"I see." She nodded in dawning understanding. "And I suppose you too are in need of an immediate heir." Her voice was deceptively calm.

"M'father's past his prime," he defended. "Make you a countess someday."

"And of course you had no wish to survey the Marriage Mart for an eligible female," she pursued.

"No. I ain't in the petticoat line."

"But somehow you saw me and that was that."

He eyed her warily now, uncertain as to where she was leading him. "I saw you at the Beresfords'."

"And, never even having danced with me, you conceived this ridiculous scheme? Really, Mr. Bascombe, but you will have to concoct a more plausible story than this."

"Dash it, I called on you once," he defended.

"Yesterday morning. And if I recall it correctly, we exchanged perhaps a half-dozen sentences. Indeed, I believe it was Juliana who spoke the most." She fixed him with a disbelieving look. "Tell me, Mr. Bascombe, how is it that you did not fix your interest with her? Could it be that the three of you—Juliana, Patrick Danvers, and yourself—devised this idiotish plan?"

"No! Patrick don't know of it! And I don't even know Miss Canfield. No, I am abducting you, Miss Ashley, and I am carrying you off to France where I intend to marry you," he maintained stubbornly. "I'm eloping with you. Thought it out—a man has to get married, after all—must secure the succession and all that. You're a nice-looking female and you ain't got a family to pay off with the settlements." He glanced up furtively to see if she believed him. "Dash it, Miss Ashley! I got no address! I can't face the Marriage Mart!"

"You cannot have developed a *tendre* for me."

"But I did!"

"Tell me, Mr. Bascombe—do you wish to kiss me?"

Bertie's eyes widened in dismay and he swallowed hard before nodding. "Want to marry you in France."

A gleam of amusement crept into Caroline's eyes. "But why go to France? 'Tis a long way to travel in a cramped carriage, isn't it? Why not just get a special license and stay in England?" She leaned across the seat until her face was almost even with Bertie's. "Are you certain you wish to kiss me, Mr. Bascombe? I do not believe for an instant that you do."

"Of course I want to kiss you! I mean, in the course of things, I should expect to." Red-faced, Bertie realized he was about to be trapped into admitting his plans if he did not do something. Manfully, he leaned over and bussed Caroline's cheek. When she did not move away, he closed his eyes and gave her a quick peck on the lips. "There," he breathed triumphantly. "See?"

"Are you absolutely certain that you feel those tender passions necessary for marriage, Mr. Bascombe?"

"Absolutely. But we have to go to France."

"Why?" she demanded bluntly. "How do you propose to marry me in a Catholic country?"

"Dash it! I left a note for Lady Canfield explaining I was eloping to France with you!"

Her amusement turned to indignation on the instant. "You did what?" she asked awfully. "Mr. Bascombe, how could you? I shall be turned off! I . . . I shall be ruined! Of all the feather-brained, idiotish things!"

Stung, he flared back, "It ain't idiotish! You'll come back a married lady, I swear!"

"Mr. Bascombe," she managed in a calmer voice, "it isn't too late. Take me back now and perhaps I can explain that it was some sort of a jest."

"Can't."

"Are you still persisting with this Banbury tale that you are wishful of marrying me?"

"Determined to do it," he maintained stubbornly. "Got to."

"Mr. Bascombe, this has gone quite far enough. If

you do not set me down this instant, I shall scream my lungs out and let you explain to the constable how you have attempted to abduct me.''

"Closed carriage—cannot be heard.''

"I can make you nigh deaf trying,'' she threatened.

"I ain't going to set you down and I ain't going to take you back, Miss Ashley. I'm taking you to France to get married.''

"Mr. Bascombe, have you thought of what a positive harridan I shall be if you force me to wed with you? I shall make your life absolutely, totally miserable. I shall give you no peace. I—''

"No, you won't,'' Bertie cut in. "For one thing, I won't listen to it, and for another, I'll just do what half the *ton* does. I'll pack you off to the country until you are glad to see me.''

"I shall spend all your money.''

"Put you on an allowance,'' he shot back smugly.

"Mr. Bascombe, if you persist in this nonsense, I shall still refuse to give my vows. Moreover, I shall do my best to escape, and I shall see to it that you are clapped up in Hoxton or some other asylum for the criminally insane. You clearly are not in possession of your wits.''

"I ain't worried.'' Resolutely he turned to stare out the window again. "I just hope Patrick gets back from Newmarket,'' he muttered under his breath.

6

It was nightfall by the time Patrick reached London. Bone-weary, he'd ordered a cold collation instead of supper, and sat down to eat it while his bath was drawn. He ought to be in a better frame of mind, he chided himself as he cut into a slab of chilled beef, for his trip to Newmarked had yielded him two things—four hundred pounds in winnings and new hope. The widowed sister of his host had shown a marked interest in him, and it had been more than that speculative gleam he usually got from women who merely wanted a little dalliance. Not that he was interested in Anthea, of course. But then, if a perfectly respectable widow dared converse with him, then perhaps not all was lost. His thoughts turned to Caroline Ashley. Now, if he'd been received, if he were somehow respectable, perhaps she would not have been so precipitate in her refusal. That refusal still stung. Devil Danvers! He'd heard the appellation a hundred times, but it sounded different coming from men. And what could she know of him, anyway? Resolutely he put her from his mind and reached for the correspondence tray.

He sifted through the usual assortment of tradesmen's bills, a letter from an antiquities scholar, and a theater subscription before Bertie's envelope caught his attention. He picked it up, examined the irregular handwriting on the front of the envelope, and sighed. Poor Bertie. Knowing him was somewhat like owning an untrainable pup—one came to feel responsible for him. Not that Bertie had not proven himself a hundred times during Patrick's troubles, of course. But Bertie's miserable attempts at writing defied patience, and Patrick was in no mood to attempt unraveling and piecing together the puzzle of his letter. He set it aside while he poured himself a glass of port.

He pushed his plate away and leaned back in his chair to prop his booted feet up on a stool. Sipping his wine, he stared speculatively at the letter, wondering what on earth Bertie needed now. He'd been gone only two and a half days, but it didn't take Bertie long to get into a scrape. With another sigh of resignation, Patrick tore open the envelope and drew out the paper inside. Absently he pulled the brace of candles closer.

Reading a few lines, he was making no sense of it until he got to what appeared to be some sort of reference to Caroline Ashley. Cursing Bertie's miserable spelling and cramped style, Patrick deciphered the words "France," "follow," and "abduction," all spelled incorrectly. "What the deuce," Patrick muttered as he tried to piece together Bertie's meaning. The letter now had his full attention as it dawned on him that Bascombe had abducted Caroline Ashley for whatever reason and carried her off to France.

"The fool—the bloody fool!" Patrick exploded. "Damn his interference! Of all the cork-brained—" He stopped and reread the offending message again in the hope he'd misunderstood it. "Damn him! Crump!" he called out as he lurched to his feet. "Crump!"

"Milord?" the butler responded promptly.

"Tell Jenkins to pack for France—I leave within the hour."

"But, your lordship—"

"I know, I know," Patrick muttered further, "I've

but got here and the horses are tired. Tell Barnes to hitch the bays instead, if you will . . . and Crump . . .''

"Yes, milord?"

"Best have Mrs. Winters pack something that'll keep—I doubt I have time to stop anywhere to eat."

"Begging your pardon for asking, sir—but is something amiss?"

"I have not killed anybody—yet—if that is what you are asking, Crump. But I cannot vouch for what I'll do when I catch up to the wretch.'' Patrick caught the butler's curious expression and snapped, "Well, do not be standing here gaping, man—I've a long way to go tonight!"

Abovestairs, Jenkins greeted the news with consternation. "Tonight?" he wailed. "But we've just arrived! And his bath—I've had his bath drawn! Are you sure you heard him aright, Crump? An hour! And did his lordship tell you if I am to go?"

"I wouldn't be using that tone around him if I was you," the butler warned, "for he's not in the best of tempers, I can tell you. And don't be asking foolish questions neither, 'cause I've not got the answers.''

"But—"

" 'Tell Jenkins to pack for France—I leave within the hour.' Them's his exact words, my good fellow—and that's all I know. Now, I have to find Barnes.''

"Should have stayed with Tillotson," the valet grumbled. "He wasn't given to queer starts. France! I hate the Frenchies—bunch of babblin' fools! And I don't suppose he said what he wanted to wear, did he? No, of course he did not!" he answered himself. "Humph!"

At almost that same moment, Albert Bascombe's other letter was being discovered some six blocks away at the Canfield residence. Caroline's absence had already been remarked, and Juliana, to avoid further conflict between her companion and her mother, had contrived to explain that Caro had been called away to her godmother's bedside. When questioned at length by Lady Lenore, she had invented in great detail the nature of the godmother's illness, but alas, could not exactly remember the lady's name. Thus, when Thomas, the footman, let it be known that Mr. Bascombe had sent a message, Juliana wasted no time in pocketing it and slipping away to her room, where, to her dismay, she found she could not read it. Since it was by then quite dark, she was becoming increasingly apprehensive about Caroline's whereabouts, so much so that she pleaded the headache to escape accompanying Lady Lenore to a select musicale at the Harringtons'.

Her mother surveyed her shrewdly, decided that she did look a trifle peaked, and thereupon bundled her off to bed. Pastilles were burned and her room was darkened to alleviate her headache before Lady Lenore left. But as soon as she heard the carriage leave the drive, Juliana wrapped herself in one of the downstairs maids' cloaks and slipped out the servants' door in search of Patrick.

By the light of day the six blocks did not seem so long, but in the dark they were quite another matter. Juliana drew the cloak closer and let the hood slip down to hide her face. Keeping her head low, she stayed to the inside away from the street and walked briskly. As usual, the night was misty from the spring rains, and she expected the damp fog to ensure her anonymity.

" 'Ere, 'ere—wot's this? Eh, Billy, 'hit's a Lunnon dove!" someone called out.

"B'leve yer got th' bloody right o' hit, yer has," a drunken companion agreed. " 'Ere, lovey—let's 'ave a look ter yer."

Alarmed, Juliana walked faster, only to hear the thud of footsteps behind her. She pulled away as bold hands grasped the cloak and it came off to expose her fashionably cropped blond curls and her blue crepe walking dress under a lantern.

"Gor! Yer ever see th' likes o' this, Billy?"

"Take your hands off me," Juliana ordered with a bravado she did not feel. "I'll call the watch."

"Yer 'ear 'er? She'll call th' watch!" the other one guffawed. "And th' watch be tippin' a pint somewheres, Oy wager! 'Ere—let's 'ave a peep, Oy say!"

"My father is Maximillian Canfield—Sir Maximillian Canfield—and he'll have you arrested . . . or transported. He will! Don't you dare touch me!"

One of the men grasped her chin and tilted her head to the lantern light. Juliana bobbed slightly and sank her teeth into the soft fatty tissue beween his thumb and forefinger. He howled in pain and released her to shake his hand. The other fellow caught her from behind and slid an arm around her neck. She stomped his foot and kicked backward furiously. For a moment she thought he meant to choke her, and she struggled with all the force in her slender body. Suddenly he stiffened and his grasp slackened.

"Unhand the lady," came a perfectly level but totally chilling voice from somewhere behind her.

"Now, guvnor—"

She drove an elbow into her captor's middle and spun around accusingly as he stepped back. "Blackguard! Miscreant! Toad!"

"Ravisher?" that voice supplied, this time with the barest hint of amusement. "Really, my dear child, but what can one expect alone and untended on a city street at night?"

"I am not a child!" Juliana snapped. "And these men—"

"I am perfectly aware of what they were about, miss." The voice had grown cold again. "Do you want me to kill them for you?"

"Now, guvnor—naught's 'armed—hit ain't! Oy wasn't ter 'urt 'er, Oy swear!" The fellow who'd held Juliana backed away, his face a pasty yellow gray in the flickering light. "Oy swear!"

The other man who had accosted her took the

opportunity to run, and his footsteps faded rapidly into the mists. "Coward!" she shot after him before turning to her rescuer. "You let him get away!" Then she saw the gleam of his rapier resting against the remaining offender's neck vein, and her eyes widened.

"Well?"

As angry and frightened as she was, Juliana still had no wish to see anybody's throat slit. "No"—she shook her head decisively—"let the watch have him. Papa will . . ." Her voice trailed off as she realized that she dared not ever let her father know of it. Her eyes traveled from the fellow who'd held her to the man behind him. "Much as it distresses me," she admitted, " 'twould be best if you just let him go."

The blade made a brief swishing sound as it sliced through the air and into flesh. The fellow screeched and Juliana closed her eyes to keep from fainting. When she opened them cautiously, he was holding a gash closed on his cheek and blood was dripping between his fingers.

"A reminder merely that one does not accost females of Quality, no matter how stupid they may be," the tall man bit off precisely as he sheathed the rapier. "Count yourself fortunate that she didn't ask for the ultimate penalty."

"M-my thanks, sir," she managed. "Had you not come—"

"Had I not chanced by, your virtue would be extinct," he finished baldly. "As it is, how can you be sure that I am any better than those louts?" He gestured at the retreating figure of Juliana's captor. "Tell me, Miss Canfield, how is it that Sir Max allows you out unprotected?"

"You know my name."

"I heard you shout it to your most recent acquaintances," he admitted.

"Then you have the advantage of me, sir," she acknowledged stiffly.

"I am Rotherfield."

Rotherfield. Juliana blinked and stared anew as she digested this startling revelation. The notorious Earl of Rotherfield. Even in the faint illumination of the street lantern, her shock must have been evident.

"Alas, yes," he murmured as he executed a mocking bow. "My shocking reputation precedes me—as always."

"N-no—not precisely, that is. I mean, of course I have heard of you, my lord. But it doesn't signify to me —I daresay you cannot be all I have heard, after all. Ten to one, you are like my cousin Patrick, and half of it is untrue."

"Patrick?"

"Patrick Danvers—Westover. He's my cousin, you know, and he's nothing like people think he is." She caught the arrested expression in his black eyes. "Well, he isn't!"

"I am certain he is not." His eyes met hers for a brief moment, and Juliana's heart lurched. "I know Bridlington."

"Then you must know Patrick's no murderer! Why cannot everyone accept the inquest verdict? Why—"

"You seem to have an uncommon concern for your cousin," Rotherfield cut in dryly. "Can it be that you were planning an assignation, perhaps? How very careless of him if he lets you wander about at night alone." His voice dropped to a silky softness. "After all, one can never be certain whom one might meet."

"It was no such thing. Patrick will tell you we should not suit—thought I do find him fascinating . . ." She caught herself and dug into a pocket for Bascombe's letter. "Lud, how I do rattle on like a noddy, sir. I am on my way to Patrick's to see if he can make any sense of this."

"At this hour?" A black eyebrow lifted skeptically. "Really, my dear, but it won't fadge. No, I think you should be at home under the watchful eye of a parent, child.''

"You wouldn't!" Juliana gasped in alarm. "And I am not a child—I am eighteen!''

"No, I wouldn't,'' he admitted with a faint smile. "I should have a devil of a time explaining to your father how you came to be in my care, shouldn't I? I mean merely to take you back and let you slip unnoticed into your parents' house. You can do that, can you not?''

"Yes, but . . . Oh, you do not understand! I have to see Patrick! Dare I trust you, sir? I mean, you would not betray a lady, would you?'' She wavered while trying to fathom his expression. "Well, would you?''

"Miss Canfield, I am scarce the person to ask.'' His dark eyes considered her for a long moment, and then he sighed. "But . . . no, I would not.''

"Then will you help me, sir? I mean, I must find Patrick, for I am afraid something ill has befallen my companion.'' Abruptly she stopped to hold out the letter. "Do you know Albert Bascombe? He's Haverstoke's heir. Well, this afternoon he took Miss Ashley— my companion—for a drive in the park. Oh, dear, I do not know what to think—Lord Rotherfield, she has not returned home! And . . . and they are barely acquainted! Surely if something had befallen, we would have heard! And then Mr. Bascombe sent this letter round to my mother, but I took it from the tray.''

"You removed your mother's letter?'' Again the black eyebrow shot upward, but his eyes betrayed amusement. "Dear me, but you are a resourceful child, are you not?''

"If I have to tell you I am not a child one more time, Lord Rotherfield, I shall shout it!'' she retorted with asperity. "And I could not let Mama see it in case it should reflect on Caro—Mama dislikes Caro and would have turned her off just this week but for Papa's intervention. You see, Patrick was trying to fix his interest with Caro.''

"Caro?"

"Miss Ashley. Anyway, I have tried to read Mr. Bascombe's letter in hopes that it will tell of her whereabouts, but I cannot make sense of it."

"Knowing Bertie Bascombe, I should not be surprised," the earl sighed. "Here . . ." He held out his hand for the envelope. "I cannot read in this light, Miss Canfield, but I've left my horses standing round the corner. If you are not afraid I will molest you, I suggest we repair to my carriage and examine this by the lamps. I can see what I think while I am taking you home."

"No!" Juliana bit her lip and drew back. "I assure you, my lord, that I am not the least afraid of you, but I must find Patrick! He will know what to do—and I cannot return home until I know what has happened to Caro!"

"You cannot walk the streets of London at night, child." A faint smile curved at the corner of a very sensuous mouth. "Alas, my lamentable memory—you are not a child."

"You are laughing at me, sir," she managed stiffly.

"Your pardon. 'Twas not my intent, I assure you. Perhaps eighteen just seems a bit young to one nearing thirty."

"Thirty? I'd thought from all I have heard—" She caught herself and flushed. "That is to say—"

"You expected me to be twice that from the life I have led," he finished for her. "While dissipation may jade the mind, my dear, it does nothing to the years."

"Oh, I did not mean that! I meant that thirty does not seem so very old. Mama has been encouraging Lord Conniston's suit, and he's above forty, so I think thirty positively young."

"You relieve my mind. Now that we have established that I am not in my dotage, perhaps we'd best consider the matter at hand. I cannot in all conscience allow you to wander the streets unattended, Miss Canfield. If you will but allow me to take this letter, I shall seek out your cousin after I've taken you home. Perhaps between us, Westover and I can determine just what has befallen your companion.''

"But I—"

"You will slip back into your house unnoted, if you can," he finished firmly, "and I will send a message round in the morning. In the meantime, you will explain Miss Ashley's absence as best you can."

"I told Mama that she was called away to her sick godmother's bedside," Juliana admitted.

"Somehow, that does not surprise me in the least. You certainly appear to be an inventive chit." His dark eyes traveled over her, and then he shook his head. "One could almost pity Lenore Canfield." He held out his arm for her to take. "But come—I've not all night to stand here, Miss Canfield."

"Wait!" She drew back indecisively. "You are not being merely patronizing, are you? You will see Patrick and you will help me find Miss Ashley, won't you?"

"I mean to attempt it."

"Will you call on me to tell me what you find? I mean, I cannot ask questions of a letter, can I?"

"I should not think I would be welcomed," he answered with a strange, unfathomable expression.

"Oh, I daresay Mama will have palpitations," Juliana admitted candidly, "but I should like it excessively, sir."

7

"You blackguard! You bloody blackguard! You miserable cur!"

"I say, Pat—you ain't mad at me, are you?"

"*Mad*? 'Tis you who are mad! I am *furious*! Bertie, how dare you do such a thing?"

"Patrick, I—"

"Of all the contemptible . . . the reprehensible things I have ever heard, Bertie, this is surely the worst! To abduct a female—any female—is bad enough, but you have chosen one whose very living depends on respectability!"

Awakened by the quarrel in the taproom below, Caroline clasped her hands to her aching temples and tried to sit up. She had no idea where she was or how she'd gotten there. Indeed, her last recollection had been of a packed supper shared in stony silence in Albert Bascombe's carriage. And that awful, hideous wine. She looked down slowly to her wrinkled gown and realized anew that she'd been abducted.

"But, Patrick, I did it for you!" Bascombe tried to explain.

"If you mean to tell me she came willingly, I'll not believe it! Heir to an earldom or no, I refuse to believe she'd prefer you to me, Bertie! But I'll tell you one thing —I'll see to it that you marry her!''

"Patrick, no! You ain't listening to me! I did it for you!''

"For me? How the devil do you explain that? Bertie, I am not getting you out of this one!''

Caroline lurched to her feet while the room spun around her. The ache in her head intensified to a steady throb as she groped her way to the door. The bitter wine seemed to rise from her stomach.

"Listen, Patrick,'' Bertie pleaded, "I don't want to marry her—I ain't in the petticoat line, for one thing, but if I was, she'd be the last female I'd take. Patrick, she tried to have me taken up by the constable at Dover,'' he babbled, "and it was a near thing, I can tell you. I had to tell 'em she was queer in the attic and that I was Haverstoke's heir before they'd believe me. How, how do you think that's going to look to m'father if he gets wind of it? And she ain't comfortable when she gets angry, Pat—she's deuced strong-minded! I had to give her m'mother's sleeping draft in the wine, else I'd never got her across!'' he finished indignantly.

"You drugged Miss Ashley? Bertie, I ought to call you out over this!''

"I told you—I did it for you!''

"Whether either of you cares a jot or not, I'd as lief not have my name or circumstance bandied about in a common taproom.''

Both men gasped at the picture she presented at the top of the stairs. Her hair was in disarray, her dress was crumpled from sleep and travel, and she was obviously not well. She started to take a step down, swayed, clutched the stair post, and closed her eyes. Patrick took the stairs two at a time to reach her before she fell. Circling her waist with his arm, he lifted her effortlessly and turned to the open door of her chamber.

"Please . . . set me down. I am . . .'' She covered her mouth suddenly and swallowed hard to combat the rising nausea before finishing, "I am about to disgrace myself."

"Lud! Here . . ." He strode quickly to the washbasin before setting her down. "Bertie!" he bawled over his shoulder. "Fetch a wet cloth—now!"

Caroline found herself in the ignominious position of being held while she retched over the bowl. Perspiration damped the tendrils of hair that escaped her coiled braids. Her hands gripped the edge of the washstand. Patrick steadied her with one arm while he dipped his handkerchief in the water pitcher and mopped her brow. When the sickness finally passed, she leaned shakily against the wooden stand to catch her breath.

"Is she all right, Pat?" Bertie asked as he finally arrived with the wet cloth.

"Of course she is not all right!" Patrick snapped back. "She's deuced sick! What the devil did you give her, anyway?"

"I told you—m'mother's sleeping draft that Knighton prescribed—it ain't poison or anything. Couldn't remember though if it was one part to three parts, or three parts to one."

"What did you give her?"

"Half and half."

"Please, I am all right now," Caroline managed shakily. "If you would but unhand me, I should like to sit down."

"No." Patrick shook his head. "You ought to be abed. If you will but lean a little, I'll help you to lie down."

"My lord, 'tis unseemly."

"Miss Ashley, this is no time for instruction in deportment. Either lean or I'll carry you." Without waiting for a decision, he lifted her again and deposited her on the bed. "Any fool can see your head must ache like the very devil, my dear, and there's no help for it but sleep and mayhap a little watered wine."

"Ugh! I shall never drink the vile stuff again," she

told him with feeling. "I should prefer a little tea later, I think."

"Please yourself." He shrugged. "I find the wine helps, but I recommend sleep most of all." He leaned down to pull the coverlet up over her dress. As he tucked it under her chin, his hazel eyes were serious. "And do not worry, Miss Ashley—I mean to see that there is no scandal."

Caroline did not go to sleep for some time after he'd closed the door. Albert Bascombe's assertion that he'd abducted her for Patrick echoed in her aching head as she tried to make sense of it. Slowly there evolved in her mind the conviction that somehow Patrick Danvers was the root of all her troubles. And despite his kindness to her, she could not forget his awful reputation as a cold-blooded duelist and a dangerous man. When she finally did drift toward sleep, when she reached that hazy nether world, her rational thoughts were obscured by images of the handsome viscount.

As for Patrick himself, his anger had dissipated enough to turn to the more real problem of what to do with Caroline Ashley. Returning to the taproom with Bertie, he ordered a bottle of the landlord's best burgundy and repaired to a corner to discuss the matter.

"Never so glad to see anyone in my life," Bertie insisted despite their recent quarrel. "Can't understand a word these Frenchies say, Pat. Don't know what they think about Miss Ashley, 'cause I couldn't even make 'em understand what happened to her."

Patrick poured himself a glass and drained it before announcing flatly, "You are obliged to marry her."

"Me?" Bertie choked on his wine and indulged in a severe coughing fit. "I say, Patrick, I ain't! No! Daresay she's a real lady, but dash it, she ain't comfortable! Once she realized I wasn't funning, she cut up a devil of a dust! Screamed for help at every inn and posting house between London and Dover—I swear she did. Didn't mean to make her sick, but I didn't have a choice. No, I ain't marrying her—not when I abducted her for you." Bertie took a more cautious sip and fixed Patrick with a baleful eye. "Dash it, but you must have got my letter!"

"I could not make sense of it."

"Thing is, you got to have a wife, ain't you? And you was interested in Miss Ashley, wasn't you? Well, I got her for you," Bertie reasoned triumphantly. "Plain as a pikestaff, ain't it? I abduct her, treat her abominably, and you rescue her—see? Her rep's in shreds, so she takes you instead of me. Bound to—won't want a slowtop like me if she can have a handsome fellow like you."

"No."

"*No*?" Bertie choked. "Patrick, you've no notion of what I've been through! No? If that ain't ungrateful!"

"For one thing, Albert Bascombe, I am not so desperate that I must needs abduct an innocent female." Patrick bit off each word. "For another, even if Miss Ashley could be brought to your reasoning, I have no use for a reluctant bride. What am I supposed to do with her? Even I stop short of ravishing females. I need a wife willing to give me an heir."

"She'll come round in a trice. I mean, you've got looks! You can turn her up sweet if you try."

"Thank you, old fellow—your confidence in my ability to correct the situation overwhelms me," Patrick muttered sarcastically. "But suppose that given the choice between us, she should choose you."

"No!" Bertie recoiled in horror. "She would not! She don't like me above half—she don't! If you could have heard her read my character in the carriage!"

"Females say a lot of things when they are angry, Bertie, and although she would not take you under normal circumstances, it's quite possible that she'd rather have a respectable fool than a rumored murderer."

"Egad!"

"And there is much to be said for an amiable husband, after all."

"No! I ain't amiable!" Visibly shaken, Bertie poured himself another glass. "I say—you're funning with me, ain't you?"

"Not at all."

"But your wager . . . Charlie . . ."

Patrick stared into the dregs in his glass for a moment and then raised his eyes to meet Bertie's. "If I am leg-shackled as a result of this, 'twill be a matter of honor rather than some stupid wager."

"Oh, lud!" Bertie groaned. "I've made a mull of it, haven't I? I just thought—"

"I know what you thought," Patrick interrupted in a gentler tone, "but it cannot work. Think on it—I've a devil of a reputation to live down, one that I doubtless deserve—how's it to look if I add abducting respectable females to my countless other sins? And Caroline Ashley's made it abundantly clear that I am not the stuff of her girlish dreams." Abruptly he rose and kicked back the chair. "The devil's in it, Bertie—she'll have to take one of us, won't she?" He stretched his tall frame and flexed tired muscles. "I've had little sleep since Newmarket—I think I'll take to my bed once I am certain she's all right."

Bertie watched miserably as Patrick moved with unaccustomed slowness toward the taproom door. Nothing ever seemed to go the way he wanted it to go. For all his pains, he'd merely endured the worst trip of his life, had ruined an innocent female's life, and had angered his only friend. Morosely he poured himself another glass and stared into the ruby liquid. Life was most unfair.

Patrick trudged wearily upstairs and slipped unnoticed into Caroline Ashley's chamber to stare down on her sleeping form. She lay in deep shadows cast by the all-too-faint glow of a single flickering candle. He moved to the nearby table, picked up the candle, and carried it closer to the bed to study her. Asleep, she appeared far less than her three-and-twenty years and far more vulnerable. She was curled up on her side, her head cradled against her palm, in much the same fashion as a child. Strands of dark hair escaped the confines of once neat braids and fell in disarray across her forehead and cheek, softening the effect of the severe hairstyle. Long lashes fringed darkly against pale, smooth skin that glowed peach in the candlelight. She was tall and slender, he knew, but in sleep she seemed small and fragile.

The anger and pique he'd felt at the refusal of his suit was gone now, replaced by curiously mixed feelings. He'd never really wanted a wife, and yet the girl was possessed with qualities he admired. Her life was as empty of hope as his own, but she'd made of it what she could, while he'd chosen to withdraw to salve his wounds. She had no illusions as to what the future held for her, but she had enough pride and spirit to refuse to sell her body into a bloodless marriage, while he'd been prepared to marry for a stupid wager. How very ironic that they should be thrust together again by a perverse fate to face a society that would exact a price she could not afford to pay or demand a marriage. A bloodless marriage.

With a sigh, he turned away and dropped wearily into a chair. He could count on his fingers the hours he'd slept in the past three days, and yet he was too tired to sleep. Setting the candlestick on a bedside table, he reached into his pocket and drew out a dilapidated translation of Homer to read of bloodier, more heroic times when men and gods conversed.

When Caroline awoke some hours later, the candle was gutted, but the room was light. Outside, ostlers in the innyard called to one another as they went about their duties, while inside, only the sound of even breathing broke the stillness. She sat up with a start and winced at the pain in her head. Then, with a jolt to her consciousness, she realized she was not alone. Patrick Danvers sat a few feet away from her, his chair leaned back against the wall, his open book on his lap. He was fast asleep.

She slid off the bed and smoothed down the skirt of her wrinkled dress before waking him. "What are you doing in my chamber, my lord?" she demanded as she reached to touch his shoulder. The memory of her sickness flashed through her mind and she recalled his prompt assistance. She shook him gently.

"My lord."

"Uhhhhhh?" The chair came down heavily as he slowly opened his eyes and blinked in the light. Passing his hand across them and then down over the rough stubble of his beard, he suppressed a yawn.

Fascinated by this close glimpse of the male animal, Caroline stepped back and waited. Used to observing the very correctly attired, excessively polite men of the *ton*, she was acutely aware that this one was different. Those hazel eyes of his met hers as a slow, rueful grin of recognition spread over his face.

"Your pardon, Miss Ashley—I must have fallen asleep."

"You shouldn't be here," she observed foolishly. "People—"

"Will talk?" he finished for her. "As we are in Calais, I doubt we will be remarked or that the *on-dit* will spread to London."

She colored at his tone of voice. "No, I suppose it will not. I daresay that there the news will be that I've gotten my clutches into Mr. Bascombe and have persuaded him to elope with me. He left Lady Canfield a note, after all."

"Miss Ashley, if it bore any resemblance to the one he left me, I daresay my Aunt Lenore will not have the least notion of what has happened. I assure you that my arrival here was the merest luck, and I have far more experience reading Bertie's letters than anyone else."

He rose to face her. "Rest assured, Miss Ashley, that I'll not let the scandalmongers devour you."

"Of course you will not—I've not the least doubt that you and Mr. Bascombe plotted my ruin, Lord Westover. For some obtuse reason, you have chosen to bring me down to your level, haven't you?"

The bitterness in her voice took him aback. "I had nothing to do with the entire affair, Miss Ashley," he retorted. "As far as I was concerned, your rather pointed refusal of my suit marked the end of any discourse between us."

"No." She shook her head. " 'Tis all of a piece. Out of pique, you have ruined me. In the space of two days, you and Mr. Bascombe have taken my reputation, and in doing so, you have taken my livelihood—I shall never be able to seek respectable employment again. I knew from the start that the abduction was all a hum—Albert Bascombe has no more interest in me than I have in him, which is none at all."

"He did it in the mistaken notion that he was helping me."

"And neither of you cares that you have taken my living!" She paced the floor away from him. "If I were a man—"

"But you are not," he reminded her reasonably. "And I do care—else I'd not be here. Once I'd deciphered his intent, Miss Ashley, I left the comfort of my house and the promise of my bed to take off in the middle of the night. Counting a trip to Newmarket, I've spent the better part of three days in a carriage, Miss Ashley. I've not had a bath or a bed in that time, so I fail to see how you can blame me. Nonetheless, I am prepared to take responsibility for Bertie's misguided actions." He moved behind her and gripped her shoulders. "You say I am to blame for your ruin. That being the case, ma'am, I am afraid you will have to marry me, after all." He felt her body stiffen beneath his hands. "I apologize for the inconvenience, since you have made it plain that I am not the sort of husband you would have, but I shall contrive to behave honorably to you."

"Marry you!" Caro choked. "Marry you! I should rather be thought the veriest trollop than be condemned to life with you, my lord! I have not the least doubt 'twas you who contrived this entire absurd situation!"

"You are mistaken!" Patrick snapped back. "But nonetheless, marriage is the only answer. As a matter of honor, I will not allow you to be ruined. Whether I knew his intention or not, 'twas for me he did it, I repeat that I am prepared to accept the responsibility. You will, of course, marry me," he finished flatly.

"I will not!"

"You will!"

"I think you are insane!"

"You are not a fool, I think," he managed more calmly. "If you find you cannot stomach me as a husband, I'll not make any demands on you." He forcibly turned her to face him. "If I can find a Protestant divine in this place, we can be married at once and return to London before Aunt Lenore even suspects what has happened." A small, wry smile played at the corners of his mouth. "You will not find me ungenerous, my dear."

"Really?" she asked with deceptive sweetness. "And what of your required heir?"

"Given the circumstances, Miss Ashley, I am prepared to forgo the necessary intimacy." His fingers dug into her shoulders and he leaned closer. Her eyes widened for a moment and then closed defensively. "I am not even fool enough to attempt kissing you again," he muttered as he suddenly released her and thrust her away from him.

"You cannot do this. I will not . . ."

He bent to retrieve his copy of the *Iliad*. "Here—

'twill give you something to read until I return." For a brief moment his eyes met hers and locked with them. "Make no mistake about it, Miss Ashley—you are my responsibility now."

8

Caroline looked up as Patrick entered the private breakfast room. Bathed, shaved, and attired casually in a soft white cotton shirt, buff-colored pantaloons, and impeccably polished black Hessians, he looked more like a man about to go shooting than a guest at an inn. His dark red hair had been merely brushed rather than arranged, giving him an almost boyish appearance. The faint but pleasant odor of Hungary water floated across the table as he sat down.

"May I join you, Miss Ashley?"

"It would appear you already have, my lord."

"Patrick," he corrected with a smile that lit the beautiful hazel eyes. "As I am but lately come into the title, I find myself looking around for someone else when I am addressed as 'my lord.' " Before she could draw back, he reached across the table and clasped her hand. "Come—can we not cry friends, my dear? I would not be forever at daggers drawn with you over something neither of us can help."

She dropped her eyes self-consciously to where his fingers held hers and was much struck by both the warmth and the reassuring strength of them. As if aware of her thoughts, he gave her hand a quick squeeze but did not release it. Involuntarily she glanced up again.

He was watching her intently. The thought crossed her mind that a mortal man ought not to have eyes like that. Finally she managed a smile and nodded. "I ripped up at you like the veriest harridan, didn't I? The more I think on it now that my head has cleared, the more likely it seems that Mr. Bascombe's brain cooked up this entire situation. You were so kind when I was ill, and yet I was out of reason cross."

"Nonsense. You had a devil of a head, my dear—I should not have quarreled with you."

"Well," she admitted, "I am willing to cry friends if you will not persist in the ridiculous notion that we should wed. Upon reflection, I do not believe the situation is irretrievable. I daresay I can contrive to come about if I can but get back to England." Catching his expression of patent skepticism, she added, "I mean, if you will but advance me the money for passage, I shall go back and apply to Miss Richards."

"No, it won't fadge, my dear." He released her hand and leaned back. "Come—am I that difficult to take?"

"No," she admitted frankly, "but we should not suit. Were it not for . . ." She groped for the right words.

"My shocking reputation?" he supplied.

"I was about to say that we are of different natures, sir. You see," she explained slowly, "in spite of my straitened circumstances, I have always harbored the insane notion that I should like to be loved and cherished by the man I marry. I . . . I cannot . . . I will not accept anything less." A wry smile formed at the corners of her mouth. "Foolish of me to cling to such nonsense, isn't it? For every rational thought tells me 'twill never happen. After all, it isn't like any gentlemen dangle after a penniless female whose father killed himself. But let us speak no more of such things, sir." Abruptly she reached for her reticule and drew out the slim, worn, leather-covered volume. "Here—I enjoyed it very much, particularly your marginal notes."

He took the book with a sigh. "You know, Miss

Ashley, I once was a dreamer also. I loved stories of bold adventure and wars. I still do, but now I know the difference between the romance and the reality of life. When I was sent down from Oxford for one of my innumerable pranks, Uncle Vernon bought me my colors. One taste of Boney was enough to disabuse me of the glory of it.''

"You fought the French? I thought—"

"You thought I merely killed my fellow Englishmen,'' he finished dryly. "Alas, my military career was short and not particularly distinguished, my dear. I took a wound three months into the campaign and was sent home to effect a complete recovery. Considering the losses we sustained, I count myself fortunate.''

"I'm sorry. I did not know.''

"My point, Miss Ashley, is that life is not like one's dreams. We do not get what we wish for. I'd like to tell you that you have a chance to get what you want, but you do not. Under the circumstances, you'd best settle for me.''

"My lord—"

"Patrick.''

They were interrupted by a serving maid bearing the breakfast tray. Reluctantly Caroline abandoned what could only lead to another quarrel with the viscount. Unfolding her napkin to lay it in her lap, she dipped her spoon to stir the cup of steaming chocolate placed in front of her.

"It would be advisable if you do not go out at all while we are here, my dear,'' he continued when they were alone again. "While we are far from London, this is a frequented port, and I have already observed other English staying in this inn. I do not think I have to tell you it would not do for them to discover your presence, particularly since I mean to give out that we eloped from Aunt Lenore's to my hunting box in Berkshire. If she brings up Bertie's letter, I'll say he was party to the elopement.''

"Where is Mr. Bascombe?" she asked uncomfortably.

"I sent him to inquire of an English divine rumored to be traveling with a Mrs. Wanstead and her son. Monsieur Crespin, our innkeeper, tells me they left for Paris yesterday, but I have hopes of Bertie's catching them. Mrs. Wanstead, it seems, is an invalid and travels quite slowly."

"Oh."

"Would you care for some sausages?" He pushed a plate toward her.

"No, thank you. I rarely have more than toast or a sweet bun in the morning."

"You aren't one of those females who never eat a morsel, are you?"

"Not at all."

He began cutting up the food on his plate. "Well, I would not have you fainting on me. Rumor has it that 'tis the fashion to starve to improve the female form, but you are quite thin enough. Here . . ." He slathered jam on a slice of bread and passed it across to her. "I do not like to eat alone."

Conversation ebbed for several minutes as they ate. Finally he wiped his mouth with his napkin. "I told Madame Crespin that your bags were lost in passage, and she is attempting to procure some dresses for you. When we return to England, I'll take you to Madame Cecile's for a fitting."

"My lord, I cannot accept clothing from you."

"Is it so very difficult to say 'Patrick'?" he asked as he ignored her refusal. "Pat-rick—'tis a simple Scottish name I got from my grandfather on m'mother's side. Try it."

"Very well. Patrick, I cannot accept clothing from you."

"I believe it's expected to clothe one's wife," he continued, unperturbed. "And it does not appear that you will be coming to me with much of a trousseau, after all. Besides," he added with a smile, "I should like to see you in decent gowns. I've been looking at you, and I've a notion that you are far prettier than I suspected at first. Take your hair, for instance—you've got it parted and braided and you still look nice. Who knows—with it cropped and curled, you might look even better.''

"Of all the stubborn, pigheaded people—'' She caught herself and managed in a more conciliatory tone, "My . . . Patrick, I cannot . . . I will not marry you—not so much because of your reputation, but rather because it is unnecessary.''

He rose from the table to stare for a moment out into the busy innyard. Turning back around to face her, he told her quietly, "Whether you choose to believe it or not, Caroline, I never killed anyone I did not have to. If that makes me repulsive in your eyes, I am sorry for it.''

"Please, Patrick—''

"I never cared much what anybody thought. I knew what I'd done, and I accepted the responsibility for my actions. I've killed three men in duels, Miss Ashley, and all with good reason. Twice I was acquitted and once no charges were brought. I don't know if that makes any difference to you or not—I don't even know what you've heard of me—but that is the truth.'' He moved to stand over her. "And in spite of all you may have heard, I am not without honor.''

"Patrick!'' Bertie burst in the door. "Your pardon, Miss Ashley.'' Turning back to Patrick, Bertie announced breathlessly, "I found him for you, and he'll do it. He won't come back, but they ain't gone but ten miles.''

"You found the Wanstead party?''

"Uh-huh. Told 'em you was eloping with Miss Ashley —long-standing passion, and all that.''

"Bertie, your heretofore undiscovered powers of invention amaze me,'' Patrick approved.

"I won't . . . I won't do it—'tis folly,'' Caroline insisted stubbornly.

Neither man paid any attention to her flat refusal.

Bertie described his meeting with the Wanstead chaplain and laid out the agreed plans. "Well, Miss Ashley"—Patrick nodded to her—"you are about to be abducted again, it would seem. As soon as I locate Madame Crespin and get you a decent wedding dress, we'll set out after the Wansteads. Bertie will see to the hiring of a carriage, since I had to leave mine at Dover. Then, once he has supported us through this ordeal, he can part company. In the meantime, you will prepare to leave this afternoon."

Once his plans were set, Patrick escorted her back to her small chamber. At the door, he stopped and chucked her under the chin. "Buck up, my dear. I mean to take good care of you, I swear."

For a time after he left, she sat staring absently into space while contemplating what to do. She had been responsible for herself since the age of fifteen—she had faced her unpleasant lot in life and made the decisions that enabled her to survive in a world where money and position were everything. She could take a certain pride that she'd earned her bread rather than hung on someone else's sleeve. Of course, there'd been no sleeve to hang on, she reminded herself, so the choice had not been entirely her own. Now she could not go back to the Canfields—Lady Lenore would see to that. And it was not certain that Miss Richards would take her back if it were known she'd traveled to France in the company of Albert Bascombe. That she had not gone willingly would have no bearing on the matter—compromised was compromised, regardless of how it came about. The only honorable outcome would be a marriage to Bascombe, and the very thought sent a shudder of distaste through her. After all, who could wish to be married to a fool, no matter how rich or how amiable that fool might be. She could just see herself trying to discuss anything of import with him. Unless he was speaking of Patrick Danvers, he had next to nothing to say. Patrick Danvers—aye, there was the rub.

Despite Danvers' reputation, she could not deny an attraction to him. Certainly she would be hard put to find a more handsome man, and she had to own that there was more to him than looks. After all, she could scarce imagine any buck of the *ton* holding her over a basin as he had done. No, there was something about him—something she could not quite fathom—that puzzled her. There was no question that he'd earned the reputation he had—he'd admitted as much; and yet . . . yet there was a gentleness, a humanity about him that she found surprising. After all, how many people would tolerate an Albert Bascombe, no matter how devoted Bascombe proved to be? Yet Patrick Danvers seemed to count him a responsibility. A responsibility. And now he would count her a responsibility too. Well, she did not want to be anyone's responsibility—not now, not ever. When she married—if she married—she wanted to be her husband's lasting passion rather than his burden.

Her thoughts turned to his first proposal, the bloodless bargain he'd offered—his name for an heir. She'd been astounded and offended by the preposterous offer. Now he merely offered his name and his protection for nothing. Somehow, it was no comfort to know that he would not expect any intimacy beween them. No, not even on those terms would she marry him.

Resolutely she reached for her reticule and drew out her purse to count its pitiful contents. It was not much, but perhaps it would pay her fare somewhere until she could find employment. She squared her shoulders and stiffened her resolve. The sooner she acted, the better it would be for her peace of mind. She would simply slip out while Lord Westover and Mr. Bascombe were gone, and she would book passage back to England before they found her.

That decided, she threw on her pelisse and tied her chip-straw hat under her chin before cautiously making her way downstairs. The taproom and entry were empty except for servants cleaning and setting up for nuncheon. It was an easy thing to slip past them and out into the bustling innyard. A large black carriage blocked her view of the street as its owner haggled with the ostlers over stable fees. It was obvious to Caroline that the gentleman was in a hurry, for he finally flung several coins on the ground. Shouting his desire to reach Paris quickly, he brushed past his waiting coachman. When he stepped out of the way, Caroline was dismayed to see Patrick Danvers returning. Almost without thinking, she caught up to the carriage door and burst out, "Would you be so kind as to take me up, sir? My . . . my great-aunt lies very ill some few miles down this road and I must get to her," she invented rapidly.

Apparently her French was sufficient, for the gentleman inside reached a hand to help her up. She settled against the squabs in time to see Lord Westover carry a box into the inn she'd left. The carriage lurched forward as the driver cracked his whip. Caroline leaned her head back and closed her eyes for a moment. She had removed herself from Patrick Danvers' insistent protection.

9

Patrick collided with Bascombe on his way out and exploded, "Bertie, she's bolted!"

"Bolted? I say, Pat, she ain't! No—can't have." His friend was positive. "I mean, she ain't got nowhere to go!"

"Nonetheless, she's gone—fled without a trace."

There was a disappointment in Patrick's voice that gave Bertie pause. "Thought you was marryin' her because you was obliged to, Pat. Seems to me that she's saving us a lot of trouble, if you was to ask me." He caught the wrath that flashed in Patrick's eyes and drew back defensively. "Look, if she don't want you and she don't want me, I don't see what we can do about it."

"Let me remind you, Bertie, that you brought her here—you are responsible if anything happens to her."

"*Me*? Patrick, it was a mistake! Thought you wanted her—I did! Now, if it ain't like that and she's gone, I say good riddance. You wasn't the one that had to listen to her coming over."

"I've got to find her."

"Why? If she's run away, seems to me we ain't got any obligation."

"Call it a matter of honor—I cannot have her out there somewhere, alone and unprotected, in a foreign country."

"A man'd think you was wantin' to marry her, Patrick."

"Maybe I do."

"For Charlie's wager." Bertie nodded.

"No. We're wasting time. You go down to the wharves and ask about today's packets to England. I'm going to ask the ostlers if they saw anything."

"*Monsieur! Monsieur le vicomte!*" Crespin called out to them. "She left with DeVere!" Panting, the fat balding man caught up. "Jean saw her leave with DeVere."

"DeVere?"

"A pig—a foul pig!"

"What does he mean?" Bertie asked when he couldn't follow the Frenchman's words.

"How did they leave?" Patrick demanded grimly of the landlord.

"Jean says they left for Paris in Monsieur DeVere's carriage but a few minutes ago."

"Paris?" Bertie howled at the only word he recognized. "Why the devil would she do that? Pat, it's all a hum! Ten to one, she's booked passage back."

"With what? I doubt she has any money," Patrick retorted.

"Pat, if she prefers DeVere, I don't see—" For an instant, Bertie thought he was about to be struck. He recoiled defensively. "But if you are determined—"

"I am. Which coach did you hire?"

"That one, but . . ." Bertie's sentence died on his lips. Westover was already halfway across the innyard. "Patrick! Patrick! You ain't even got your coat! What the devil d'you think you can do? Oh, all right!" Bertie threw up his hands in disgust and took off at an undignified lope after him. "Patrick! Patrick! I say, you ain't driving, are you?" he yelled.

"The devil I'm not!" Patrick called down from the box.

"Oh, lud!" Bertie groaned. Catching sight of the

astonished driver and coachman, he shook his head.
"Better ride inside or else hang on, I can tell you."
Muttering, he heaved his slender body up into the hired
carriage. When they climbed up on the box with his
lordship, Bascombe just shook his head. "Fools."
Resigned to what could only be a wild ride, Bertie barely
had time to settle in and get a firm grip on the pulls
before the carriage took off. As the team of horses
lunged forward, he held on for dear life. Patrick drove
to an inch, he knew, but this was no road to
Newmarket.

More than a mile ahead of them, Caroline was having
her own doubts. A closer inspection of her traveling
host proved to be somewhat unsettling. For several
minutes, he'd stared speculatively at her with small
deep-set eyes that she mistrusted. Finally she'd feigned
sleep to escape his close scrutiny. To her horror, she felt
him slide across to sit beside her. When his hand slid up
the sleeve of her worn pelisse, her eyes flew open. He'd
removed his coat and neckcloth.

"You will not find me ungenerous, *mademoiselle*."

Somehow, his words rang differently than Patrick
Danvers' had. She stiffened like a stone statue and
stared studiously out the carriage window, hoping that
aloofness would be sufficient rebuff. It wasn't. A nasty
little laugh assailed her ears as he moved closer.

"Come, *mademoiselle*—do not play the innocent
with me."

"You are mistaken, sir," she retorted coldly. "I am
not that sort of female."

"You wish to be coy, perhaps?" he asked with a
softness that sent chills down her spine. "Very well,
mademoiselle—DeVere accepts the challenge." His
hand snaked out to grasp her chin and force it upward.
"You are passably pretty, after all, and it's a long way
to Paris."

The smell of stale garlic and soured wine on his breath
nauseated her, but she could not turn away. Her

stomach felt like lead as his face blurred her vision with its closeness. The oddly detached thought that he had bad teeth crossed her mind a fraction of a second before she felt the crushing force of his lips on hers. She clenched her teeth against the outrage of his probing tongue and twisted her head in his grasp. His free hand slid up her back to press against her spine painfully. Her fingers crept to her chip-straw hat, found the decorative pin, and withdrew it. His teeth gnashed against hers for possession of her mouth. She struggled for a moment and then plunged the hatpin into his thigh with all the force she could muster.

He drew back, howling in pain. Infuriated now, he slapped her so hard across the face that her head snapped backward and her hat came untied. "You like these little amusements, English?" he panted as he gripped her shoulders painfully and shook her. "DeVere sets the rules here, I think."

"Take your hands off me else I shall scream," she threatened with a calm she did not feel.

"Scream, *mademoiselle.*" He shrugged. "My men are used to it."

"I'll have you arrested for this."

He fixed her with those nasty deep-set eyes. "Who's to know?" he asked with that chillingly soft voice of his before he lunged to pin her back against the corner of the coach seat with his body. "Do not come the innocent with me—I have heard about English women."

"I assure you that . . . mmmmumph—"

Her protest was cut short as he took possession of her mouth, gagging her with his tongue. The chip-straw hat fell to the carriage floor. The grim reality of his intent mobilized every defense Caroline had. She clawed at his face with her fingernails, bucked and struggled beneath his weight, and felt along the seat for the hatpin. For answer, he imprisoned her arms at her sides and began trailing wet, slobbery kisses down her neck. She twisted and turned, flailing helplessly against the arm that held her. When he returned his attention to her mouth, she sant her teeth into the soft fullness of his lower lip and bit as hard as she could. He screamed and slapped her again. She grabbed a pullstrap and tried to swing across the seat away from him. His hand caught at her pelisse, ripping it literally off her back.

"You beast!" she seethed indignantly. "Look what you have done. You've—" Angry, impotent tears flooded her eyes. " 'Tis my only—"

He flung the ruined coat onto the floor and lunged again to force her against the squabs. Bent on conquest rather than seduction, he explored her body roughly with his hands, squeezing her breasts painfully through the material of her dress. She kicked and flailed to no avail against his greater strength. When he found the buttons that lined her bodice a hindrance to his eager fingers, he caught at the neckline and pulled viciously until the fabric of both zona and dress tore away, exposing her white breasts. As he bent his mouth to bite, she clutched a handful of his hair and yanked him away. Abruptly the carriage jerked to a stop, sending Caroline and her tormentor to the floor in a tangle of arms and legs.

Before she could right herself, Caroline saw the carriage door wrenched open and looked up into Patrick Danvers' hazel eyes. His gaze traveled over her bare breasts and then turned wrathfully to the now cowering DeVere.

"Get out!"

"*Monsieur*—"

"Thank God you are arrived," Caroline breathed in relief as she tried to cover herself. "He . . . he . . ." She choked at Westover's expression.

"I am aware of what he attempted," Patrick cut in harshly. "DeVere, defend yourself!"

"*Monsieur*—" The Frenchman read danger in the other man's eyes.

"Out!"

"You find me unarmed!"

"You are as armed as Miss Ashley!" Patrick shot back.

DeVere shrank back against the floor. "*Mais non!*"

"Aye," Patrick growled as he reached to pull him up by the lapels of his coat. With a mixture of horror and fascination, Caroline stared as the Frenchman rose before her eyes and then disappeared through the open door. Patrick flung him to the ground below and stood over him with clenched fists.

"*Pitié, s'il vous plaît! Pitié!*" DeVere shielded his face against Patrick's grim stare.

"I'll show you what you would have shown her."

"*Non!*"

"Exactly."

"I will not fight!" DeVere shouted defiantly.

"No?" Patrick strode purposefully to his hired coach and took down the carriage whip. DeVere, sensing his intent, scrambled for the safety of his own coach. The whip cracked, catching him as his foot gained the step, and he screamed as he fell. "Unless you wish to be whipped to ribbons, you'll choose your weapon." The leather whirred through the air to snap loudly again as it cut into DeVere's shirt. "Surely you carry a sword or a pistol, Monsieur DeVere."

"Take her—she's nothing to me," the Frenchman begged. "For God's sake—"

The whip cut like a knife again, turning words into a high-pitched scream of terror that trailed off into a pitiful whimper. DeVere rolled up into a huddled ball in the dirt. Patrick raised his arm and sent the lash cracking again and again until the back of the Frenchman's shirt was laced with red.

"Stop it!" Caroline clutched her torn pelisse against her chest and jumped down. "Stop it—you'll kill him!" Coming up behind Patrick, she caught at his right arm.

He looked down, first at her and then back to where DeVere lay babbling incoherently in the road. Shaking his arm free of her grasp, he walked to turn the Frenchman over with his booted toe. "By rights, I ought to kill you for what you would do to a defenseless female," he growled.

"Defenseless? Defenseless?" DeVere screeched indignantly. "*Monsieur*, she is a tigress!"

Ignoring him, Patrick's eyes met Caroline's. "You are unhurt? If the bloody cur's harmed you, I'll kill him."

DeVere cried out in alarm, but Caroline shook her head. "No, my lord, I am all right, but I cannot thank you sufficiently for—"

"Patrick," he cut in.

For some unfathomable reason—maybe it was the way he was looking at her or maybe it was the relief of being delivered—but for some reason, Caroline felt the urge to cry. "Patrick." She nodded through a mist of tears as he enfolded her comfortingly in his arms and cradled her head against his chest.

DeVere, sensing that he would not be missed, took the opportunity to edge on his hands and knees to his carriage. Once there, he scrambled up the step and slammed the door. His bemused driver and coachmen continued to stare at the wild English lord until their master tapped impatiently on the roof of the passenger compartment. Reluctantly the driver raised his whip over the team. Once the carriage began to roll forward, DeVere stuck his head out the window and yelled at Patrick, "I wish you joy of her, my lord!"

Patrick's eyes dropped to the torn pelisse Caroline held in front of her, and she colored as she followed his gaze downward. Without a word, he released her to unbutton his shirt. Shrugging out of it, he handed it to her.

Her eyes widened at the sight of his bared chest with its darkly curling hair, and then were averted. "I . . . I could not take your shirt, my . . . Patrick. 'Tis unseemly."

"Unless you wish to provide Bertie with a rather

fetching glimpse of the female person, Caroline, I think
you had best take it. Come . . ." He reached for her
hand and led her behind the rented coach. "There's
none to see you here. I'll go on and roust Bertie while
you cover yourself."

She waited until the carriage obscured his vision and
then dropped the pelisse. Surveying the damage to her
dress, she came to the sad conclusion that it was hopelessly ruined and she now quite literally had nothing to
wear. With a sigh, she drew on the white cotton shirt
and buttoned it at the neck. It swallowed her up and the
sleeves hung down over her hands, but his generosity
was not lost on her. Feeling the warmth that still
lingered from his body, she gathered the shirt closely
about her and rolled the sleeves. He must surely feel as
foolish as she if he meant to go back like that.

"I say, Pat—you ain't serious!" Bertie's plaintive
whine floated back to her.

"I am. You'll have to ride on the box."

"But why? I ain't—"

"Her dress is torn, and I doubt that my shirt will
cover her enough."

"But what's that to say? I mean, I ain't going to
look—I swear."

"Bertie—"

"Oh, all right! I wish we'd never heard of the chit!
Females! Deuced nuisances, if you was to ask me!"

"I daresay she's no more fond of the association than
you are, but there's no help for it."

Caroline looked down at the shirt and was dismayed
to find that the soft material did not completely hide her
charms. There was a faint dark outline that hinted at
what lay underneath. Her face flamed anew.

"Ready, my dear?" Patrick stepped back around the
rear of the coach. "If 'tis any consolation, Caroline,"
he told her sympathetically, "you are better covered
than I. Besides, once we get back, Madame Crespin has
located another gown for you."

"But I . . ." She had started to say that she could not accept clothing from him, but given the condition of her only dress, she realized she would have to swallow her pride and take what he provided.

His eyes met hers. "Exactly so."

He handed her up into the coach and then swung up beside her. Leaning down to reach under the seat, he drew out a rolled carriage rug, spread it out, and draped it around his shoulders. Settling back, he took in her disheveled hair and his cotton shirt. He managed a crooked smile that twisted one corner of his mouth and shook his head. "What a pretty pair we must be, Caroline. I wonder if Bertie's limited powers can explain us out of this one."

"I shudder to think of what he will tell." Incredibly, she found herself answering his smile with one of her own. "My lord . . . Patrick . . ." She groped for words. "I . . . I cannot tell you how very glad I was to see you just now. If you had not come after me . . ." Her voice trailed off.

"You'd have been in the basket." He nodded. "Suffice it to say, it was a rare fright you gave me, Caroline Ashley, and I hope you know it. When I returned to the inn and you weren't there, I'd no notion of where you'd gone. If it hadn't been for Crespin, you would have disappeared without a trace."

"I know."

"I hope you do not mean to make a habit of this, my dear, for I've no wish to spend the rest of my life chasing after you. I mean, I should prefer a more comfortable life, if you do not object."

"My Lord—"

"Patrick," he corrected.

"Very well," she sighed. "Patrick, I wish you would cease this nonsense about being obliged . . . I mean . . . that is—" She looked up and was startled by the warmth of his expression.

"Caroline," he interrupted wickedly, "I think 'tis

you who are obliged now. You simply cannot take me back to that inn without my shirt and expect me to maintain a shred of reputation.''

"Stop it! You are a man, after all, and it is no such thing.''

"Must you always be so literal, my dear? Do you never wish to cut up a dust, to fall into a scrape? You know''—he leaned forward conspiratorially and lowered his voice—"I suspect you have more of a sense of adventure than you care to admit, Caro Ashley, else you'd never have chanced running away.''

"You sound much like Juliana.''

"Mayhap.''

"Well . . .'' Caroline appeared to consider. "I am not sure you are right, but then I've never had the opportunity to find out, I suppose. My father died when I was still at school, and circumstances made my choices for me.''

"And you regretted that.''

"I learned to accept it.''

"What would you do, my dear, if you suddenly found yourself possessed of a large fortune?'' he changed the subject abruptly. "I mean, how would you spend it?''

"Well, I would not run up huge tradesmen's bills, if that is what you are asking. If I had a fortune, I would hope that I would not be so self-centered that I did not wish to help other people at least a little. I mean, I cannot see using it all for social position, after all. I think that I would be concerned with education.'' She looked up to see him watching her closely. "Well,'' she defended, "before I became acquainted with you, 'twas books that gave me all the excitement in my life. I lived in my mind what I read, and I think it a pity that there are those who never have even that.''

"What? No routs, no balls?''

"I should like to go to some, I suppose,'' she mused wistfully. "But I can tell you one thing: I should have more than one decent gown." She stopped. "You are funning with me, of course."

"No." He looked out the window for a moment at the rolling countryside. "I am nearly twenty-seven, Caroline, and I am only now finding what I want."

"Now 'tis my turn to pry. What is it that you want?"

"If I told you, you would not believe me. Besides, it would all depend on my ability to reestablish my character with the *ton*."

"Oh."

Conversation lagged as each turned to his own thoughts. The swaying motion of the carriage gradually took its toll until Caroline leaned her head back into the corner and cradled her cheek against her elbow. Her ordeal with DeVere still very fresh in her mind, she could not help contrasting the lecherous Frenchman's behavior to that of the notorious Patrick Danvers. She shuddered to think of what would have happened had it not been for Westover. In that last twilight of consciousness, she remembered how very different it had felt when Patrick Danvers had kissed her.

The coach rolled and lurched along the rutted road, jostling her head against the wooden sides of the passenger compartment. Patrick watched Caroline slip deeper into sleep despite her uncomfortable position and then eased her over to rest against his shoulder.

10

Caroline dipped her pen in the ink she'd borrowed from Madame Crespin and poised it above the paper. She no longer held Patrick Danvers responsible for her plight, nor did she still consider him a totally ineligible connection. Quite the opposite, in fact, she admitted to herself as she began to write. But she simply could not marry him, particularly not since she suspected she was more than half in love with the red-haired, hazel-eyed viscount. She could not have been happy with the bloodless, purely business sort of marriage he'd first proposed in what now seemed a long-ago encounter in the Canfield parlor, but then neither could she accept his name and nothing more when it was offered merely to save her reputation. Her reputation—that was almost laughable. Aye, she'd always been above reproach, but to what end? A lonely, thankless position devoted to grooming other young women for brilliant matches. Stop it, she chided herself severely. She had to learn to accept her lot in life, else she would be miserable.

"My dear Westover," she wrote, paused, and then scratched the words out to begin anew with, "Lord Westover," only to scratch that out also. It was more difficult than she'd imagined to say farewell to the dashing Viscount Westover. "My dear Patrick," she tried again, and stopped. Too informal, she decided with a heavy sigh. Drawing a line through that, she penned "Dear Patrick Danvers," and studied that. Incredibly stupid, she guessed, but she had to start somewhere. Still dissatisfied, she crumpled the paper and took out another sheet.

This time, she forged ahead despite misgivings about how she must sound to him. "Dear Westover," she wrote finally, "I lack the words to express how very grateful I am for your assistance yesterday. I owe you a debt of gratitude that I will never have in my power to repay." She read what she'd written carefully and thought it sounded rather foolish also, but she lacked the time to polish it as she would have liked. Instead, she plunged on with, "While I am cognizant of the honor you would do me, I must still regretfully decline your offer of marriage. There is not between us those mutual feelings that are necessary for a successful union, and it would be wrong to wed without that. While you might profess yourself content with a marriage of convenience, I believe there would come a time when you would regret it. There would always be the risk that you might later form a lasting passion for another. I know that I have cherished the foolish but romantical notion that someday I will find someone to love me. What folly it would be if we were not free to follow our hearts when that happens."

Patrick Danvers' image floated before her face, and she remembered how it felt to wake up safely cradled against his shoulder. Even though she was alone now, her face flamed at how she must have looked—disheveled in torn gown and covered insufficiently with his shirt. She'd been astounded by the feel of him, warm, alive, hard-muscled, and definitely masculine. She'd never been that close to a man before—except DeVere, and that was a far different matter. No, Patrick Danvers was nothing like she had thought him.

Regretfully she dipped her pen anew. "Therefore, I am decided," she continued writing, "that my best course of action is to return to England and seek my old position at the academy where I taught before your aunt employed me. I am taking the fifty pounds you insisted on giving me for pin money, and I am using it for my passage. Once I am situated again with Miss Richards, I will contrive to return your money and I will reimburse you for the dress you bought me. It is quite the loveliest gown I have ever owned, and I shall cherish it as a reminder of your friendship." How very foolish you are, she chided herself again. There is no way that you will ever have the kind of money necessary to pay him back. She glanced down at the twilled green silk he'd bought for her wedding dress. It must have cost him the equivalent of a year of her wages, she supposed. Resolutely she turned back to the matter at hand and finished with, "While I doubt we shall ever meet again, I will never forget your kindnesses, my lord. I wish you the best of fortune in all your endeavors, and I remain Your Obedient . . ." She stopped to cross out the last word and put simply "Servant, Caroline Ashley."

Her spirits considerably lowered by the finality of her own letter, she folded the paper and sealed it with candle wax. It was over, it was done, and she was ready to get on with her life. She had not the time for regrets just now, anyway, for she could not depend on his being gone above another hour. She'd overheard him tell Bascombe that they were pressing on to catch the Wanstead party as soon as he'd taken care of a business matter. Secretly she'd suspected that he meant to buy her another gown for the trip back to London.

She propped the letter up on a chest, checked her reticule for her money, and slipped down the stairs. There was no sight of him or of Albert Bascombe. She breathed a sigh of relief as she gained the innyard undetected.

Walking briskly, she followed her nose to the bustling

docks, where she inquired as to a packet bound for Dover. Directed insolently by a fellow who promised her a better offer, she made her way to where a small ship was taking on passengers. She clutched her reticule nervously and took her place at the end of the line while hoping fervently that she would be under way before the Viscount discovered her note.

Dividing the line two people ahead of her, the ship's officer announced that there was no more space. She stared for a moment in dismay and then pushed forward.

"Please, sir, I have to get back to England—'tis of paramount importance—please." She reached into the reticule and drew out her purse. "I have the money—I can pay extra, if need be."

He took in her expensive dress and looked around for a companion. Finding none, he pushed her back. " 'Tis full."

"But you cannot be! I have to get to England—I have to!"

He looked her up and down with new interest, much in the way DeVere had done. "And you'd be grateful, wouldn't you?"

"I have money," she reminded him.

" 'Tis full then." He shrugged insolently and turned away.

"But . . . you don't understand. I—"

"I believe the young lady is with me, aren't you, my dear?" An elderly gentleman far in front had turned around to watch them. "I am sorry for the misunderstanding, but I had expected my granddaughter to be taking a later packet. Come, my dear," he addressed Caroline, "we'll send back for your luggage."

"But, your lordship," the officer expostulated, "there's no room!"

"Nonsense." The elderly gentleman dismissed him with the air of one used to being obeyed. "She will share my room, of course."

Caroline was taken aback by the sudden turn of
fortune. A quick appraisal of the old man convinced her
she had nothing to fear from him. He smiled a thin
smile of encouragement and motioned her forward.
"Well, do not be standing there, child—come give me
an arm to lean on."

"Yes, Grandpapa," she murmured obediently.

Grasping her elbow with a decidedly frail hand, he
balanced between her and his cane. "You had a pleasant
journey here, child?" he asked kindly. "You really
must tell me all about your trip."

She waited until they were safely aboard and in the
privacy of his tiny cabin before she addressed him.
"Your pardon, my lord," she began, "but you must
think—"

"At my age, my dear, I am not overly given to quick
conclusions," he interrupted with a twinkle in his faded
blue eyes.

"But you must wonder how it is that I have no
baggage and no maid, and—"

"And I am sure you will provide me with a most
edifying story, no doubt, but first I must sit down, my
dear." He pointed with his cane to the nearest chair.
"Over there." As soon as he was seated, he looked up
not unkindly and indicated a nearby seat. "Now," he
told her as she pulled it up and sat down, "you will find
me all ears, my dear. I trust you will enlighten me."

She was suddenly at a loss for words. "I am Caroline
Ashley, my lord, and—"

He nodded his head politely in acknowledgment.
"And I am Milbourne, Miss Ashley."

"The Lord Milbourne?" she asked incredulously.
"But you must be—"

"A hundred years old?" he supplied with a faint
smile. "Only seventy-five, child, and definitely no
threat to your virtue. But do go on."

" 'Twas not my meaning, sir. I meant who has not
heard of Lord Milbourne, my lord? I own I had not

expected to find you standing on a French wharf—I mean, I should expect you to be attended.''

"My servants discreetly drew back when I intervened on your behalf. They know not to get involved unless it concerns my safety, Miss Ashley. As for my reasons for being in France, they need not concern us.''

"No, sir,'' she murmured.

"Now, my dear, how is it that I find you alone and unprotected in a foreign city? Everything about you says Quality except the lack of a maid and baggage.''

She took a deep breath and nodded. "I have been abducted, my lord.''

"And abandoned?'' He shook his head sadly. "In my day, Miss Ashley, morals were not so lax, I assure you. An abduction required a marriage.''

She hesitated, unwilling to tell of Patrick Danvers or of Bertie Bascombe, and yet realizing that she owed Lord Milbourne an explanation. Apparently her thoughts were transparent, for he added gently, "If I am to help you, I must know the whole so that we may best salvage the situation. Anything you have to say will never be repeated outside this room unless you wish it.''

"Are you to help me?'' she asked hopefully. If a man of Milbourne's impeccable social standing were to come to her aid, all might not be lost.

"Most assuredly,'' he soothed. "But do go on.''

"Well, I am not precisely certain as to how it all came about, sir, but I shall attempt to tell you what I believe to have happened. I was employed by Sir Max and Lady Canfield to companion their daughter Juliana through her first Season. Through Juliana, I met her cousin, Patrick Danvers, who seems to be hanging out for an indigent but willing wife. He proposed marriage to me with the understanding that he would provide for me handsomely if I gave him an heir within the year. Needless to say, I found the proposal sordid in the extreme and I declined.''

"Naturally.'' Milbourne put his fingers together and

nodded. "Sordid in the extreme. I daresay you had not heard of the betting on the books at White's then? 'Twould seem young Patrick stands to inherit more than Golden Ball if he can produce a respectable wife and a son within a year of the reading of Vernon Danvers' will. Needless to say, the betting is heavily against him."

"I didn't know, but 'tis most unfair if 'tis so."

"He may not know of the wager at White's, but I understand it came out of a bet he made with a cousin of his the day the will was read."

"But it's not fair! How can he meet such infamous terms, sir?" she demanded indignantly. She caught the arrested expression on the old man's face and stopped.

"So you refused his suit," Lord Milbourne repeated. "His shocking reputation, I daresay, although I have suspected the fault lies with Bridlington's revenge more than with the boy."

"You know Patrick?" she asked in alarm, and then recovered. "No, 'twas not just his reputation, sir, but the fact that I could not live with such an arrangement. I mean, 'tis not as if he offered his regard even."

"It is not so much that I know young Danvers, child, but rather that I am acquainted with Lord Bridlington, a mean-spirited, vengeful person if there ever was one. But we wander, I fear. If you refused his suit, am I to collect that he abducted you?"

"Oh, no! Do you know Albert Bascombe, sir?"

"Haverstoke's heir? I have attempted conversation with the boy on several occasions, but no, I do not know him."

"Well, he abducted me."

"Bertie Bascombe?" he asked incredulously. "Now, that does surprise me, I must own. I should not suppose he had the wits for it."

"Oh, not for himself, you understand. I mean, he regards Patrick much in the light of a hero and he would do anything for him. Well, I believe he thought that if he abducted me and carried me off to France, I should be so grateful to see Patrick that I should change my mind.''

Lord Milbourne leaned forward, fascinated. "And?"

"Lord Westover—Patrick—was furious. I mistook the matter because I overheard Mr. Bascombe say he did it for Patrick, but now I believe that Lord Westover did not know of it until Mr. Bascombe left him a letter. Anyway, Mr. Bascombe made it quite clear that he'd no wish to marry me.'' She met Milbourne's curious stare and smiled ruefully. "I gave him an awful time on the way over, you see, and he had to drug me to get me on the packet.''

"He drugged you? The boy ought to be clapped up in Bedlam!'' his lordship snorted. "In my day, he'd have been called out for it!''

"Well, anyway,'' Caroline went on, "he gave me too much, and I was heartily sick when I woke up.''

"This exceeds the bounds of decency!''

"'Twas then that I realized that Lord Westover had come after us, for they quarreled in the foyer of the inn. I tried to stop them, but I was unwell, and had it not been for Patrick's assistance, I should have disgraced myself then and there. As it was, he got me back to my room before I was sick.''

"How awful for you, child.'' Lord Milbourne reached a bony hand across to pat hers. "You are safe enough now, I promise.''

"Strange—that's what Patrick said too. He said that since Mr. Bascombe abducted me for him, he felt responsible, and that he would give me the protection of his name.''

"I see—and this is when you suspected he was part of the plot?''

"Yes, particularly after what I'd overheard Mr. Bascombe say about doing it for him. Naturally, I refused his suit again. But this time, he insisted that it was a matter of honor and that I should not be expected to produce an heir.''

"How very generous of him," Milbourne observed dryly.

"Well, he was generous after a fashion, I suppose," she admitted judiciously, "for he was certain to lose his wager. Anyway, he informed me that I could go my separate way after the knot was tied, but that I would marry him. There was a small problem, however, since there is a dearth of Protestant clergy in France. Unfortunately, he managed to locate one and set about getting me a dress to be married in. While he was gone, I ran away, but my choice of companions was exceedingly poor. I fell in with a man named DeVere, and he thought . . ." She looked away quickly and her voice dropped in embarrassment. "He thought that I was not a proper sort of female. Well, he tried to molest me—and very nearly succeeded—but Patrick had followed us."

"Am I to deduce that this DeVere is deceased?"

"No—he would not meet Patrick."

"How very wise of him."

"Patrick whipped him rather badly with the coach whip, sir—I thought he meant to kill him with it."

"I'm surprised he did not."

"I grabbed his arm and held it to stop him."

"And then?"

"He let DeVere escape while he looked after me. My . . . my dress was torn rather badly, you see." Her face reddened as she remembered how she'd looked. "Patrick gave me his shirt to wear and took me back to the inn where we'd been staying. Madame Crespin, the landlord's wife, procured this dress for me with Patrick's money. It was to have been my wedding dress." She smoothed the silk twill with her fingers. " 'Tis quite the loveliest thing I ever have had."

"Child, I have the distinct feeling that you are not entirely indifferent to young Danvers. Am I right?"

"Oh, no . . . that is . . . yes," she finished lamely.

"Then why are you here?"

"Because I can no more accept a marriage of convenience than I can accept a business arrangement designed to give him an heir. There," she sighed in relief, " 'tis out in the open, sir. I fear I am a hopelessly romantical female."

"Could you not have wed with him and hoped for the best?"

She shook her head. "What if he never came to care for me?"

"I see." He crossed his legs and leaned back in his chair to study her for a moment. "I'd say young Bascombe bungled the matter badly."

"I beg your pardon?"

" 'Tis of no import. Well, my dear, 'twas an exceedingly edifying story that gives me an idea or two of my own."

"You will not betray what I've told you?" She stiffened in alarm.

"Word of honor, Miss Ashley. But I vow I've not been so diverted since my granddaughter led young Tony Barsett such a merry chase. For a time, I thought Rotherfield meant to queer the works before the marriage had a chance to work." He seemed lost in thought as he closed his eyes. For several seconds Caroline thought he meant to doze off. "No," he mused finally, "I believe I'll have to do something about this."

"But you said you would not—"

He waved aside her protest and gave her a sly smile, much like one who had suddenly come up with a new diversion. "I assure you, Miss Ashley, your secrets are safe with me."

11

"Oh, my dear, I'd no notion you even knew her! Hurry—you must wear your blue merino—oh dear . . . no, no . . . perhaps the lavender muslin would be better."

Lady Lenore, when appraised that Leah Barsett, Viscountess Lyndon, had come to pay a morning call on Juliana, was wreathed in smiles. Lady Lyndon, after all, was no less exalted a personage than Lord Milbourne's only grandchild and therefore a leader of the younger set amongst the *ton*. Not even that lady's oft-remarked association with the Earl of Rotherfield could offset Lord Milbourne's influence. The *ton*, for all its social snobbery, had long since decided that if the fiery Tony Barsett saw nothing amiss, then surely Lady Lyndon must be blameless.

"Mama," Juliana responded with unusual patience, "I have on my best sprigged muslin, after all. I am sure that Lady Lyndon would rather I was prompt than kept her waiting while I changed my dress." The girl turned over the gilt-embossed card and tried to hide her puzzlement.

"Well, I am sure that she must have remarked you at the Beresfords' . . . or mayhap 'twas the Connistons'— you were in particularly good looks there, my love. But

why ever would she pay a call on you?'' Lenore
Canfield could barely contain her curiosity. "If you
wish me to go down with you—''

"No . . . no. I mean, she asked to see me, Mama.''

"Well, do hurry, love,'' Lady Lenore admonished
her daughter, "for 'twould not do to keep Lady Lyndon
waiting. Oh, I vow I am at sixes and sevens, Juliana! If
she takes you up, you are quite made.!''

The girl bit back a retort that she considered herself
quite made anyway, for had not Lord Barrington
applied to her father for permission to pay his
addresses? Not that she meant to take him, of course,
for he was the most stolid fellow. Besides, she had
already quite set her cap for the notorious Earl of
Rotherfield.

"Juliana! Do not be standing there dreaming, love!
Lady Lyndon will think—''

"Stuff, Mama!'' Nonetheless, Juliana slipped her
mother's fringed Norwich shawl about her shoulders
and headed down.

Pausing at the door of the blue saloon, she was surprised to hear voices coming from within. After all,
Thomas had brought up but one card. She smoothed
back a rebellious gold ringlet, tucking it behind her ear,
and stepped inside. A gentleman lounging against the
mantel with his back to her turned around. She gasped.

"Your pardon for the subterfuge, Miss Canfield, but
I saw no other way. You know Lady Lyndon, of
course?''

"We have been presented.'' She nodded politely to
where Leah Barsett sat. "Oh, Lord Rotherfield, have
you found Caro?'' Wiping suddenly damp palms on the
skirt of her sprigged-muslin gown, she moved forward.

"Alas, no.'' He shook his head. " 'Twould seem that
there is not a trace of her or Bascombe, and it now
appears that your cousin has disappeared also.''

"Patrick?''

"I have been to his house twice, Miss Canfield. The

last time, I took the liberty of interviewing his servants, all of whom profess to know nothing except that he left late the night we met." He reached into his pocket and drew out Albert Bascombe's letter. "You may as well have this back, child. I find that I have reached *point non plus* in the search." His black eyes took in her dismay and his expression softened. "I am sorry, Miss Canfield. If there is anything else I can do—"

"Have you considered reporting her absence to Bow Street?" Lady Lyndon asked suddenly. "It would seem to me that you would have cause to worry."

"But I cannot! Mama thinks she is with her godmother, you see."

"Well, I am certain that Marcus has made every effort to help, but perhaps he could send discreet inquiries to the ports. Somehow, I cannot quite imagine Albert Bascombe doing anything dreadful, but—"

"Oh, would you, sir?" Juliana breathed, grateful for anything to further her acquaintance with Rotherfield. The thought echoed in her brain that if she didn't do something, didn't make a push for his attention, this incredibly handsome, fascinating man would disappear from her life before she even had a chance to attract him as a suitor. She flashed an appreciative smile at Leah Barsett. "And you are quite right, Lady Lyndon: perhaps Lord Rotherfield could . . ."

A flicker of amusement lit the black eyes as the earl recognized her ploy. "Miss Canfield, of all that can be said of Albert Bascombe, he has never been known to molest females. I daresay that the clue is in this letter, but I have not the power to decipher his scribbles. Ten to one, your companion will come about in excellent fashion."

Unbidden, tears of frustration began to well in her famed blue eyes, giving them added sparkle. Unconsciously she brushed them away and prepared to accept defeat.

It was a gesture that was not lost on the earl. As used

as he was to the wiles of the other sex, he was touched
by the artlessness of this simple human reaction. He
drew back the letter and stuffed it back in his pocket.
"All right," he agreed with a sigh, "I'll pursue the
matter further, child." Turning to Leah Barsett, he
nodded. "The only word I can make out of this whole
thing is 'France,' so perchance he took her there. I will
set inquiries afoot at Dover and see if we can trace them.
Miss Canfield, you will hear of my success or failure
either from Lady Lyndon or myself by the end of the
week."

"Oh, thank you, sir!" Juliana breathed in relief. "I
shall quite look forward to it."

"Good heavens! My salts!"

They turned to where Lenore Canfield stood clutching her bosom in shock. Lady Lyndon, used to the
reaction from her friendship with Rotherfield, was the
first to move. "Marcus," she addressed the earl, "assist
Lady Canfield to a chair if you will, please." Taking a
bottle of smelling salts from her reticule, she uncorked it
and waved it beneath Lady Lenore's nose. "There—you
are quite all right, I am sure. Her color is returning
nicely, my dear," she told Juliana as the earl steered the
shaken woman to a seat.

Juliana, who had told Rotherfield that her mother
would have palpitations, had certainly never expected
her to actually have them. After all, the woman had
never done so before. She grabbed a copy of the *Gazette*
that lay on a table and began fanning with it. "You are
quite all right, Mama—'tis the heat. May I present Lady
Lyndon? And Lord Rotherfield is but come calling with
her, after all."

Lenore Canfield looked up at the disreputable earl
with such malevolence that even he was taken aback.
"What a surprise," she managed through tightly
compressed lips.

"Yes," Leah Barsett interposed smoothly, "Marcus
is accompanying me to the Pantheon today, and I per-

suaded him to stop with me since it is quite on our way. But we really must be going, Lady Canfield, for I am told the best buys are to be obtained in the morning. Perhaps Juliana would wish to accompany us—''

"No!" Lenore choked, and then realized how she must sound to Lady Lyndon. "That is to say, I am sure it would be nice some other time." Casting a baleful eye at Rotherfield, she shook her head. "I am sure you understand, sir, that Lord Barrington has applied for Juliana's hand, and it would not do for him to think her the least bit fast. While dear Lady Lyndon may be seen with you, she is a married lady, after all, and can survive the association."

Her meaning was not lost on Leah Barsett, but instead of infuriating the lady, it appeared to amuse her. The beautiful Leah merely chuckled good-naturedly. "Alas, 'tis your dreadful rep, Marcus, that makes Tony think I am so safe with you. He knows full well I shall not be subjected to importunities from other men while in your company, I daresay." Drawing on her gloves, she nodded to him. "We really must be going, for I am determined to have some of that blue lustring and those dyed feathers I saw last week. Fanny Egglesworth assures me that they will be gone early."

As soon as they had left, Lady Lenore turned to her daughter coldly. "Make no mistake about it, miss— while an association with Lady Lyndon is desirable, one with the Earl of Rotherfield is not. I will not tolerate your casting out lures to a man of his stamp. Do you understand me, Juliana?"

"Perfectly, Mama. You would have me go about with Lady Leah, provided that Lord Rotherfield is not in attendance."

Pleased with the unusually meek tone of Juliana's voice, Lady Lenore let the matter drop. But she made up her mind that the sooner her daughter was safely and respectably married, the better.

Outside, Leah Barsett waited until the earl had joined

her in her carriage before announcing, "I like her, Marcus, but 'tis not like you to put yourself out for a child."

"It isn't, is it?" he agreed imperturbably.

12

Patrick read Caro's letter and sank into the nearest chair in a state of disbelief. "The little fool—the bloody little fool!" he muttered under his breath. "She'll ruin herself!"

Bertie took the paper unnoticed and squinted in concentration while he tried to read it. "Well"—he shook his head in disgust—"if that don't beat the Dutch! After all we have been through for her, you'd think—"

"I can't let her do it! She cannot know what 'tis like to be cut by everyone—she cannot. My reputation may have put me beyond the bounds of polite society, but I can still save her from the slanderous insults, Bertie."

"I say, Pat, you ain't going to go after her again!"

"I am."

"But—"

"Bertie, I have to! As little as I consider it to my credit, my reputation is such that there's not a man in England fool enough to insult my wife. I can spike their guns. Oh, the tabbies may talk for a month or two, but she can survive that. She cannot survive going back unwed." Resolutely Patrick rose and straightened his shoulders. "Besides, I mean to have her."

"Thought it was your honor."

"That too, but I think I could live with her—that it would be different with her than with some empty-headed ninnyhammer."

"You sound like you was head over heels," Bertie observed.

"Maybe I am."

"Well, if that's the way it is, we're wasting time. Got to find out if she was on one of the packets today. Then we just go back and find this damned school. I ain't got much stomach for another abduction, mind you, but if you're set on it, well, then I guess I ain't above helping you. But if I was you, I'd just find her and tell her you've thrown your hat over the windmill for her," he added practically. "I would."

"Bertie, sometimes you are a prince." Patrick grinned in spite of himself

"I say, Pat, I ain't! A friend, that's all."

Many times in the following days, Bertie regretted his offer of help. The search was fruitless from the beginning. After being unable to determine that she had actually crossed the Channel, they'd combed Calais before returning to Dover. No ship's master on either side of the Channel could recall an unattended female of Caroline's description. Having remembered that Juliana's school was in Shropshire, Patrick dragged Bertie there only to find that Miss Richards had not seen her since she left to go with the Canfields, and she had not heard from her in weeks. Now at a total loss, they turned back to London, arriving well after dark.

As his carriage turned down Curzon Street toward his house, Patrick still could not admit defeat. At the corner to the Canfield residence, he struck his palm in inspiration and told Bertie to call on Juliana. Rapping on the ceiling to gain his driver's attention, he had the carriage halted.

"Me?" Bertie howled as though stuck. "I say, Pat, I can't! I mean, 'twas me that abducted her! They ain't going to let me in the door, I tell you. I'll be clapped up in Newgate—if I ain't taken straight to Bedlam! No!''

Patrick leaned back in his seat and played absently with the rapier he kept in the coach. Bowing the thin blade with his hands, he let it go and it quavered in the air. ''No?'' The famous Danvers eyebrow shot up quizzically. ''Bertie, we have not come this far to quit. You abducted Caroline Ashley from this house—you have a debt of honor to determine her safety. If she has been able to get back into my aunt's house, my presence could well put her out on her ear.''

''Besides, it's night! Can't call on a female at night. Won't be home anyway.'' Bertie could see he was making no impression. ''Bound to be out—Incomparable, after all—asked everywhere,'' he continued desperately. ''And if they was home, they know I left with Miss Ashley. How can I go back and ask where she is? They'll think I've done something to her. And if she's there, no telling what she's told 'em—they might send for the constable!''

''Bertie—''

''You do it.''

''My patience is at an end, Bertie.''

''But I made off with her!''

''If you left a note anything like the one you left me, I promise you they had not the least notion of what happened,'' Patrick responded dryly.

''Pat, I can't talk to your cousin—I can't. Ain't in the petticoat line—I ain't! Wouldn't know what to say to her!''

''Bertie—''

Bascombe could see it was useless. Capitulating gracelessly, he flung himself down from the coach and presented himself at the Canfield door. To his horror, the butler did not turn him away, and a footman was sent to inform Miss Canfield of his presence. When she came down, he could only stare.

''What have you done with Caro?'' she demanded as soon as she'd closed the door behind her.

"Thought you'd be out," he blurted foolishly.

"You came calling on me because you thought I was out?" she asked incredulously. "Mr. Bascombe, are you quite all right?"

"If you mean I'm touched in my upper works," he retorted stiffly, "I ain't. But Patrick sent me to ask if you'd heard from Miss Ashley. I can tell you ain't heard either, so I'll go."

"May I remind you she left with you. What have you done with her, you fiend?" Juliana stepped in front of him to bar his way. "Well?"

"Me? I ain't done nothing!"

"She cannot have just disappeared, sir. We have not seen her since she left with you almost two weeks ago. You have your brass coming here to ask for her, Mr. Bascombe. I think the Runners would be interested in what you have done with her."

"I told you—I ain't done nothing!"

"Where did you take her?"

"Took her to Calais, but it ain't like you think, Miss Canfield—I swear! Patrick—"

"My cousin would not be a party to an abduction," Juliana cut in coldly, "and Caroline Ashley would not have willingly run off with you. Where is she?"

"Oh, what the devil?" Bertie wavered a moment, squirming beneath Juliana's implacable stare. "Miss Canfield, I abducted Miss Ashley in hopes that Patrick would come after her and they could make a match of it. Just wanted to help, that's all. But she bolted—and we ain't seen her since?"

"What?"

"We ain't seen her since. Patrick's half out of his mind over it, too. Stupid thing for me to do, but deuced silly of her to run off."

"Patrick knew of this?" she demanded awfully. "I don't believe you, Mr. Bascombe."

"Of course he didn't know it! Left him a note—like the one I left you. Mad as fire, too. She ran away, saying she was going back to that damnable school, but she ain't there. Miss Canfield," Bertie explained plaintively, "we been all over England looking for her."

"Well, she is not here. I didn't know what happened to her, so I told Mama she'd gone to care for her sick godmother." She sank onto a settee and sighed. "Before long, Mama's going to demand to know where she is, Mr. Bascombe."

Bertie shuddered. The thought of Lady Canfield's wrath coming down on his head was frightening. "Tell her someplace up north," he offered.

"Where? Besides, that does not help Caro. If she's not here and not with Miss Richards, something's happened to her—something dreadful. Mr. Bascombe, you've got to find her."

"Me?"

The door opened suddenly to admit Lady Canfield. Juliana jumped guiltily at the sight of her mother bearing purposefully down on her. Bertie clutched his beaver hat helplessly. Suddenly Lady Lenore's face inexplicably lightened, and she held out her hand to him.

"Mr. Bascombe—dear Mr. Bascombe—for shame, coming here for a little *tête-à-tête* with my daughter behind my back." Incredibly, her face was wreathed in smiles. While Bertie goggled in confusion, she turned to Juliana. "You sly puss! Now I know why you were so adamant about Barrington, my love, and rightly so, I might add."

"Mama—"

"Ah, Mr. Bascombe," Lady Canfield continued rapturously, "does the earl know you are here?"

"M'father?" Bertie furrowed his brow and tried to make sense of her conversation. "Well, no, but—"

"Then why are you here?" she asked bluntly as the smile thinned.

"Uh . . . attached to Miss Canfield—that's it," Bertie groped helplessly. "Uh . . . had to see her . . . highest regard . . . lud . . ."

His disjointed and confused explanation brought a

gleam to that avaricious lady's eye. "Well, I very much regret that Juliana's father is out of town, but I daresay 'twill not matter. After all, I am certain he would not stand in your way."

"Uh . . ." Bertie stared in dismay.

"Mama!"

"Oh, I quite count Mr. Bascombe as one of the family, my love." Lady Lenore dismissed Juliana's indignant expression with a wave of her hand. "Countess of Haverstoke! La, what a triumph for you both! You are indeed a fortunate young man, Mr. Bascombe, for I take leave to tell you she is a most unexceptional girl. But then I daresay you know that, after all."

"Uh . . . most unexceptional . . . but—"

"Under other circumstances, I could not approve your being here unattended at this hour, but I expect this calls for a celebration. Thomas!" she called out as she rang the bell pull. "Some of Sir Max's best wine! 'Tisn't every day that one's only daughter is betrothed!"

"Mama!" Juliana howled. "It is no such—"

"Hush, love! A little maidenly reserve is one thing, but I can assure you Mr. Bascombe will make you an amiable husband, won't you, Mr. Bascombe?"

"No! That is to say, Miss Canfield is a very good sort of female, I am sure, but—"

"Mama, stop this!"

Lady Lenore's smile faded. She fixed Bertie with a penetrating gaze that made him squirm. "Mr. Bascombe, I will not have my daughter's affections trifled with! You have come calling at an unreasonable hour, you have contrived to see Juliana alone, and you obviously stand on intimate terms with her. As a fond parent, I should not like to think the worst of you."

"Oh, I assure you that—"

"Good. Then we are agreed. Once the announcement has appeared in the *Gazette*, Sir Max will contact you about the arrangements. You will not find us overly demanding, I think.''

"Mama, I won't!"

"Nonsense, my dear. Here is Thomas, after all." Taking one of the filled glasses from the silver tray, Lady Lenore lifted it in triumph. "To my daughter—the future Countess of Haverstoke!"

"Lady Canfield," Bertie tried desperately as a glass was thrust into his hand, "I—"

"Sir Max and I could not be more pleased, I assure you."

Tears welled in Juliana's eyes until they brimmed. "Oh, Mama, how *could* you?" she wailed.

"I say, Lady Canfield, if she don't—"

"Nonsense. She is overset merely—a common occurrence when one contemplates the married state. She will be fine, Mr. Bascombe."

"Mama," Juliana managed as she brushed aside an errant tear, "would you mind so very much if I spoke to Mr. Bascombe alone? As we are now betrothed, I daresay there cannot be any objection."

Lady Lenore, well aware of what she'd accomplished, hesitated. "But I fail to see the necessity—"

"Please, Mama."

"At this hour, I cannot allow you above five minutes, young lady," Lady Lenore capitulated finally. "I am sure Mr. Bascombe must be on his way."

The door had scarcely closed before Juliana rounded on the hapless Bertie. "You fool! How could you have let her do this?" Drawing herself up imperiously, she faced him and ordered, "You will cry off, of course."

"Dash it! I ain't a loose screw! How's it to look if I was to do that?"

"I don't care. Attached to me indeed! Of all the things to say to my mother, that was the stupidest, the most idiotish, the most—"

"You didn't speak up either!" he retorted.

"Well, I can tell you this: if you do not cry off, Albert

Bascombe, I'll make you sorry for it—I'll get into a scrape and you'll *have* to. I will!''

"Why don't *you* cry off? Females can do it better than men. You changed your mind—that's it—we ain't suited!"

"Obviously you do not know my mother!"

"Tell you what," Bertie placated. "I just won't puff it off to the paper. Ten to one, she'll let the matter drop in a week or two."

"Mama?" Juliana eyed him incredulously. "You jest, of course. Did you not remark her interest in the title you will have someday? My mother is the worst of the matchmaking mamas, Mr. Bascombe, and she has her clutches in you! If you do not cry off, I shudder to think of what will happen to you!" she shot back at him as she flounced out of the room.

13

Caroline closed the book gently and prepared to tiptoe from the room, but Lady Milbourne's eyes fluttered open and she reached out a bony hand to stay her.

"Don't go yet."

"I thought you were asleep."

"No—tired merely, my dear. You have given me such pleasure with your reading, Caroline," the old woman murmured. "It cannot be very pleasant for you to sit for hours with an invalid, after all."

"Actually, I enjoy reading very much." She reopened the book and searched for her place.

"No—I would speak," the elderly woman sighed. "This stupid complaint robs me of my strength but does not sap my mind." She paused a moment to consider the young woman before her and then nodded. "Yes, you remind me of my daughter Charlotte—very definitely. Oh, she had not the dark hair nor the dark eyes, but there was much about her manner that I can see in you. Marianna was the great beauty, you know, and Frances was so very social, but Charlotte was possessed of both wit and ability. Alas, they are all gone now—Marianna of the wasting fever, Frances in childbed, and Charlotte from an inflammation of the lungs."

"I am so sorry, madam," Caroline offered quietly.

"Oh, I am reconciled to the losses, my dear. At least there remains dear Leah, Marianna's daughter by Mr. Cole. You know her as Lady Lyndon, I am sure."

"Everyone knows Lady Lyndon. It was the *on-dit* of the Season when she married Viscount Lyndon."

"Two years ago that was, and a very good match it was for the both of them. Leah was the making of Tony Barsett, I can tell you, and it has proven to be a love match, after all. Oh, there was some unpleasantness about Rotherfield for a time, but it was all unfounded on Leah's side, for she was head over heels for Tony. Not that it did not give the tabbies something to speak of then. Oh, dear—how I wander, child."

"Anyone who has ever seen Lady Lyndon with her husband knows they are devoted," Caroline soothed.

Abruptly Lady Milbourne changed the subject. "Yes, well, Ned—Lord Milbourne—and I have been thinking what a pity it is that you were never afforded the opportunity of a come-out. Ned is persuaded that you must have taken on the instant you had been given the chance, my dear."

"I had no expectations, ma'am."

"Sometimes there are other things than expectations," the old woman observed. "In my day, the Gunning sisters married two dukes, and everyone knew they had nothing."

"Perhaps times have changed."

"Perhaps, but have you never wished for a come-out of your own? Have you never dreamed of grand balls, masquerades, and routs at all?" Lady Milbourne questioned.

"Who has not?" Caroline admitted. "I should imagine that even the backstairs maid must dream of such things."

"It would give Lord Milbourne and myself much pleasure to bring you out." Anne Milbourne noted Caroline's thunderstruck expression and hastened to stifle any objections. "No—do not dismiss what I am about to say, my dear, for I quite mean every word of it. It has been twenty years since last we had a girl to fire off, and yet I can remember the excitement of the Seasons as though it were yesterday. Our foolish pride robbed us of Leah's triumph when she was wed, so we did not share in her courtship or her wedding."

"But, madam—"

"Hear me out, please." Lady Milbourne took in a deep breath and lay back to gather her strength. "In the weeks you have been in our house, we can see the credit you would do us. You are a remarkable young lady, Caroline—despite every adversity, you manage to accept your lot and to make a life for yourself. We think you could do even better if you but had the opportunity. Ned and I mean to frank your Season, my dear."

Caroline shook her head. "Do not think me ungrateful, Lady Milbourne," she managed at last, "but it would be a lie for me to parade about on the Marriage Mart when I've nothing to offer. I am three-and-twenty, ma'am, and I have not even the merest competence. I should be laughed out of Almack's if I dared to put myself forward. Surely you have heard that my father was Baron Ashley, the one who put a period to his existence rather than be cast into debtors' jail."

"Well, we cannot change your age, of course,"—the elderly lady nodded sagiciously—"but we should naturally expect to provide a small settlement to make your come-out respectable. And as for your father, the blood was good even if the temperament was not. I knew your mother slightly—she was of an age with my Frances, after all."

"I could not let you do it."

"Nonsense." The faded eyes met Caroline's dark ones. "Have you met Lord Rotherfield, my dear? So handsome, in a cold sort of way—don't you think?"

"Everyone notes it, but—"

"As everyone notes his association with my granddaughter, I should imagine," Lady Milbourne added dryly.

"Most people think that Tony Barsett is not the sort of person to tolerate any impropriety and therefore reason that the friendship is a harmless one," Caroline pointed out.

"Most people." Lady Milbourne nodded. "And I've not the least doubt they are right. Tony Barsett would not tolerate infidelity, I can tell you, but that does not still the gossips. A man of Rotherfield's stamp is bound to be remarked no matter what he does. He's much like young Danvers in that respect, but he's not one to shun the society that shuns him."

"I fail to see—"

"I mean to bring you to the earl's notice, my dear—'tis time the devil took a wife."

"What?" Caroline stared, unsure as to whether she'd heard Lady Milbourne correctly. "Madam, you wish me to compete with Lady Lyndon for Lord Rotherfield's attention?" she asked incredulously.

"Not 'compete' precisely, my dear. I merely wish you to make his acquaintance. If you do not suit, of course I should expect nothing. If, on the other hand, he should fix his interest with you, and you should come to reciprocate his feelings, I cannot but think it would be a good thing for both of you."

"Madam, I couldn't."

"Well," the elderly woman admitted, "it might come to naught, or some other gentleman might take your fancy, even, and I certainly would not expect to stand in your way if that should happen. Suffice it to say, I shall count it enough to see you go about as you should."

"There is no need, I assure you. I am quite content with the arrangement Lord Milbourne made."

"Pooh. You are far too young a woman to spend your days reading to an old lady, child. Ned and I are agreed you should be with people your own age when you can. Of course, I should still enjoy your company when there's naught else for you to do."

"You cannot have considered—"

"Ah, but I have. I have spoken to Tony and Leah and they will sponsor you. It is all settled, my dear. Arrangements have been made for Leah to take you to the linen draper's this very afternoon. While Madame Cecile is far too busy this time of year, I am sure we can contrive by employing a dressmaker to come here. You do not appear to be an extravagant person, after all, so I think the result will far outweigh the expense."

The vision of new gowns was an enticing one. Patrick Danvers' observation that "with the help of a good modiste and a dresser, you'll be a credit to me" echoed in her mind. Oh, what she would not give for him to see her as she ought to be dressed. How she longed to turn his head and gain his attention rightfully rather than as an obligation or as the means to win a wager. Regretfully she shook her head.

"I would be living a falsehood, Lady Milbourne."

"Ned is decided that we shall settle one thousand pounds on you, regardless of whether Rotherfield fixes his interest with you or not. It will—"

"I could not accept it!"

Unperturbed, the elderly lady continued, "It will be in the form of a bequest, so I doubt you will be able to refuse it, child. If you find yourself unable to accept the money, 'twill be your decision as to how 'tis spent."

One thousand pounds. To someone of Lord Milbourne's immense wealth, it was a paltry sum, but to Caroline it was a fortune. She sank back in her chair and tried to assimilate the Milbournes' incredible offer.

"Come, Caroline," Lady Milbourne cajoled. " 'Twould give me such pleasure to see a girl dressed in her finery, ready for balls, routs, and masquerades again. Life holds so very little for me these days, my dear. Do not deny an old woman her fond wish for your foolish pride. Let me see you as you should be, dancing away the nights—let me hear of your triumphs, and I shall be repaid."

"I do not know what to say. I . . . I know I shall not take, but . . ."

"Well . . ." There was a faint twinkle to the faded eyes. "When you are Countess of Rotherfield, you may name your first daughter Anne for me. I should like that above all things." With an effort, she leaned forward and extended a bony finger. "The earl has been disappointed too long, my dear—'tis time he found a lady of his own. And if it should prove to be young Danvers instead, I will not cavil over it, after all." Falling back against her pillow, she added, "My Ned was a devil in his time too."

14

Patrick was the first to see the notice in the *Gazette*. When it caught his attention, he choked on his morning tea. Albert Bascombe, having shared in the excesses of a night at White's, Watier's, and Boodle's successively, ate in blissful ignorance across the table. Unable to speak from his coughing fit, Patrick merely pushed the paper under Bertie's nose.

"I say, Pat!" Bertie protested. "You know I ain't a hand to read!"

"There," Patrick directed in strangled accents as he pointed at the offending notice.

"Eh?" Bertie squinted to focus, and then the color drained from his face. "No! Why, that . . . that . . . Tartar! It ain't no such thing!"

"About to be leg-shackled, old fellow? Tut—and you did not even tell me."

"Pat, I ain't!"

"Thought you said Juliana knew nothing about Caro —you did not tell me that she swept you off your feet," Patrick murmured while suppressing a grin. "Lud, what a dance the chit will lead you."

"Wasn't to my credit to tell it," Bertie defended. "Besides, how was I to know they was going to puff it off?" His pale face creased in consternation at the thought of something. "Oh, no! Patrick, you've got to tell Miss Canfield I didn't do it!" Groaning, he reread the notice and then let the paper drop. "She ain't going to like this!"

"I take it the betrothal is not of your making?"

"Lud, no! No offense, old chap, but your cousin ain't the sort of female I'd want. Well, she ain't! Deuced strong-minded, if you ask me, and she don't like me above half. Lud! She'll be mad as fire!"

"Bertie," Patrick asked suddenly, "how did this come about? Not even my greedy aunt can force you into parson's mousetrap if you've no stomach for it."

"Much you know about it!" Bertie snorted. "There I was, trying to find out about Miss Ashley, and your cousin was ripping up at me, and then your aunt comes in and allows as how 'tis an assignation! I told you it wasn't proper to call on a female in the middle of the night, but, no, you sent me in to make a cake of myself! Couldn't think quick enough—never could—and when Lady Canfield wanted to know why I was there, I said something about regard for Miss Canfield. All at once, I was betrothed!"

"Surely there was more to it than that."

"No. She had me at *point non plus* cleaner than a broomstraw in a custard, Patrick! And then Miss Canfield ripped up at me, telling me she'd make me miserable if I didn't cry off! I'm going to look like a dashed loose screw, ain't I? I tell you, you've got to help me!"

"Bertie," Patrick soothed, "Juliana will find a way out of this coil. Do not worry for one minute that she won't, for my cousin's every bit as stubborn as I am."

"But what am I supposed to tell everybody? I don't even know the chit!"

"Well, I suggest you do the pretty and wait for her to cry off."

"Me?" Bertie howled. "Pat, I can't—got no address, for one thing."

"Believe me, Juliana will take care of it," Patrick

promised. "All you have to do is to make yourself amiable and wait."

"But what's m'father to think?"

"No doubt he'll be pleased."

The vision of the earl allied with Lady Canfield was almost more than Bertie could bear. If they both favored the match, he was probably as good as married to the vivacious Juliana, and that thought struck terror in his heart.

They were interrupted by the butler inquiring in disapproving accents if Lord Westover was at home to a young female person. Since Patrick had ended his last liaison with a fair Cyprian months before, and even if he hadn't, it would be highly improper for her to present herself at his house, he was about to have the caller sent away. Then the thought crossed his mind that Caroline Ashley, having found herself in desperate straits, might be turning to him. An unlikely circumstance, it nonetheless prompted him to direct the girl in.

Seeing she was considerably shorter than Caro, he instantly regretted the decision, and was about to order her out of his house when she pushed back the hood of a faded cloak.

"Ju!"

"Patrick, you've got to help me! Mama's determined that I shall marry Albert Bascombe, and I—"

"Ahem!" He cleared his throat and nodded toward Bertie.

Her blue eyes took in her betrothed and turned stormy. "You! You blackguard! You promised me you would not send off the notice!" she railed at him.

"He didn't," Patrick intervened. "In fact, he reacted in much the same way, Coz."

"Well, I very much doubt they would have printed it if he hadn't sent it in."

"Don't be tiresome, Ju. Bertie views his betrothal as the next thing to swinging from the Nubbin' Cheat—don't you, Bertie?"

"Don't want to be married," Bascombe insisted.

"Never did. Ain't in the petticoat line, for one thing. But your mama—"

"Mama!" Juliana breathed in dawning horror.

"Just so, Ju. Aunt Lenore left nothing to chance, did she? Ten to one, she knows Haverstoke will be delighted to see his heir settled down to a life of respectable bliss."

"Well, Haverstoke can hang! I won't do it! Mama can starve me first!"

"Lud, Ju—how gothic," Patrick murmured. "No, you need to outface your mother, my dear. If you appear too entrenched in your dislike, she'll just take you back to Crosslands, and your Season will be over, won't it?" he reasoned. "If I were you, I should appear to accept it, and then I'd approach Uncle Max to stop the wedding."

"I will not! Do you think I like having it bandied about that I am betrothed to Albert Bascombe when everyone knows he is—"

"Stop it, Ju! Do not say something you might come to regret. Just now, I'd have to say Bertie is your greatest ally, my dear. Remember, he does not want to wed with you either."

"I may be a slowtop, Miss Canfield, but at least my mother does not cast out lures to eligible *partis* for me," Bertie retorted stiffly. "And I wouldn't have you if you was the last female in England, either!"

"Oooohhh!"

"Cut line—both of you! This notice is the latest *on-dit* by now, anyway, so there's naught to be gained by carping at each other. I suggest you carry on properly until something comes up that gives one of you an opportunity to cry off."

"But this is my Season! How am I to find an eligible *parti* if I am already betrothed?" she demanded.

"Did you perhaps have someone in mind? Out with it, my girl! I've known you since you were in swaddling bands, after all. This is Patrick—remember?"

"No, of course not," Juliana lied.

"Then what's the harm in playing Aunt Lenore's little game for a while? Amuse yourself at her expense."

"I forgot you were a man—you wouldn't understand."

"Ju . . ." He reached to lift her chin with the crook of his index finger. "I do understand," he added in a gentler tone. "I think you have your heart set on someone already. Should I get him for you, I wonder?"

"You could not." She met his hazel eyes and looked away. "That is to say, there is no one, Patrick."

"I say, Pat, I can't do the pretty—I can't. I'll make a cake of myself, I will. You going to come with me to all these dashed boring affairs? Of course you ain't!" Bertie complained.

"I'll mean to go about, anyway, Bertie. How else can I hope to hear of Caroline Ashley again? Surely someone somewhere will have news of her. She cannot have just disappeared off the face of the earth."

There was something in Patrick's voice that gave Juliana pause. If he meant to face the censure of the *ton* after three years of social exile, he must surely have changed. "Patrick, you cannot mean it," she ventured. "They'll give you the cut direct, you know."

"It's been a long time, Ju," he signed. " 'Twill not be pleasant, but if Rotherfield can face them down, then so can I."

"Well—"

"I have to try—I have to find Caroline."

15

"You'll be a credit to me, my love," Leah Barsett murmured approvingly as Caroline turned before the mirror. "I had not thought it possible that Mrs. Cranston could have done so well, but full half the *ton* will want the name of your dressmaker, I promise you. I cannot wait until Marcus sees this gown—he has such impeccable taste, you know."

"Marcus?"

"Rotherfield." The beautiful Lady Lyndon leaned closer to confide, "He is not at all what you have heard of him. Even Tony has come to like him."

"Oh."

"Yes, and he is quite alone in this world—a tragedy of sorts, if you ask me."

"Well," Caroline admitted, "he seems to delight in his reputation. Indeed, he fairly flaunts it in all things. I mean, look at his clothes, his arrogant bearing, his very manners—'twould seem he tries to stand apart."

"You mistake the matter then. Twice in my recollection, the *ton* has chosen to utterly censure one of its members without true cause. In the first instant, it was Marcus Halvert; in the second, it was Patrick Danvers. In Marcus' case, he flaunted that censure, showing up where he knew he was not wanted, daring anyone to give him the cut direct, and acting for all the world as though he ruled it. He knows he is feared, he knows he is disliked, but he will not give anyone the satisfaction of seeing him retreat. He exacts a price for that censure. Lord Westover, on the other hand, appears to turn his back on those who would shun him.''

"Patrick Danvers is no coward!" The words escaped before Caroline realized how they must sound. "Your pardon, Lady Lyndon, but I did not mean—"

"Leah—you must call me Leah, for we shall be quite like sisters," Leah Barsett cut in. "And I am sure no one calls Westover a coward, my dear. You mistook my meaning. I am saying that with him 'tis a mutual dislike." She moved closer to examine the ruching along the hem of the sapphire-blue silk gown Caroline modeled. "Charming, I think. You were quite right to choose this color."

Caroline smoothed the shimmering fabric across her shoulders and turned sideways for a better glimpse of the fit in a mirror. Leah Barsett had done her job well, for everything was perfect from the soft kid slippers to the ostrich feathers that adorned Caro's cropped and curled hair. The effect, while not exactly a total transformation, certainly was arresting.

"Here"—Leah slipped a single strand of pearls around Caroline's neck—"they ought to be sapphires, but I daresay that as a maiden lady, 'twill not be remarked if you have only pearls. Your husband will provide other jewels later."

"Are you two about ready?" Anthony Barsett, Viscount Lyndon, called through the closed door.

"Just a moment," Leah answered. She reached to pinch Caro's cheeks and to pat an errant ostrich feather into place. "There—'tis perfect, love."

Tony Barsett beamed when they came out. "Well, I shall be the most remarked fellow at the Connistons' tonight, I think, if I can but persuade both of you to hang on my arms. I can hear that damned poet Maria keeps dangling on her skirts—ten to one, he'll bellow out that I've balanced the fair goddess with a dark one."

"Fiddle," Caro announced succinctly.

"Caroline does not succumb to extravagant compliments, Tony." Leah smiled.

"You relieve my mind." He grinned back.

"What she means, my lord, is that I am not a totally green girl, I think." Caroline looked from the viscount to his lady and wondered how Lady Milbourne could have ever worried. It was obvious that the Barsetts were a devoted pair.

"Tony, do you mind very much that I have asked Marcus to accompany us?" Leah asked suddenly.

"Oh-ho! So that's the lay of the land, is it? No, of course not, my dear, but don't you think that a little transparent?" He met his wife's warning look and retreated. "I mean, does he know what you are about?"

"Tony!"

"Rotherfield has been a bachelor for nearly thirty years, Leah," he reminded her. "It won't be as easy to lead him into parson's mousetrap as you think. Besides, I think he's still more than half in love with you."

"Tony!"

Caroline could feel the color flood her face and wondered just how much Tony Barsett knew of Lady Milbourne's plans. To hide her embarrassment, she raised her ostrich-plume fan and began to exercise it vigorously to cool her face. After hearing Lady Lyndon's remarks on the subject, she could not decide whether it was she or the earl that was the true object of their matrimonial machinations.

"Ah, well, here's where you put it to the touch, Leah," Tony leaned over and whispered to his lady. "I believe Crowley is admitting Rotherfield now."

They were at the top of the stairs when the door opened in the foyer. Caroline looked down at the same moment the earl looked up, and she thought she saw a hint of amusement in eyes so dark they appeared black. As usual, his dress was affected, with everything black but the stark white of his plain shirt and his cravat. From raven hair to gleaming highlows, he was austere in the extreme. Only the winking of diamond studs and stickpin broke the utter plainness of his clothing. Not that his dress did not speak of elegance and expense, of course, for every article was the pride of his select tailor.

Tony Barsett gave each lady an elbow and swept them down the wide staircase in the grand manner. Caroline felt rather like she was going to a court presentation instead of a mere ball. Rotherfield kissed Leah's extended fingers before turning to bow over Caro's hand.

"You have the advantage of me, my dear—I cannot place the acquaintance," he murmured politely as his lips brushed over her demiglove.

"Caroline, may I present the Earl of Rotherfield," Leah announced helpfully. "And, Marcus, this is Caroline Ashley."

His fingers seemed to tense on hers for a moment, but his face never betrayed anything. The black eyes met hers. "Miss Ashley."

"We have been presented once, I think, but I daresay the affair was such a shocking squeeze that you could not possibly remember it."

"Caroline is staying with Grandmama and Grandpapa, Marcus. I believe her mother was some sort of goddaughter to my grandmother."

"Ah, the ailing godmother then," he mused almost to himself. To Caro he smiled apologetically. "Nonetheless, I should be called to book for forgetting such a lovely lady."

The carriage ride was taken up with the merest commonplaces, and Caroline began to relax. There was nothing in Rotherfield's manner that gave evidence that he knew of the Milbournes' plans. Indeed, it seemed that he was patently but politely disinterested until they were set down at the Connistons' doorstep. Lord Lyndon escorted his wife, leaving the earl to take Caro inside. Tucking her arm in the crook of his elbow, he leaned slightly to whisper, "You intrigue me, Miss Ashley. Really, but I should be interested to hear how you came to Milbourne House, my dear."

He led her through the receiving line with a determination that made her marvel. Ahead of them, Lord and Lady Lyndon could be heard to remark that the extra card they'd requested was for Lord Rotherfield and Miss Ashley. There was a certain coolness, betrayed by a thinning of Lady Conniston's smile, but she merely nodded perfunctorily and extended two fingers toward the earl. After all, if the Lyndons could take him up, she supposed she would have to endure. Turning to Caroline, she furrowed her brow as though to place her. "Ashley? I do not believe I have the pleasure of your acquaintance . . . Oh, dear, how stupid of me," she recollected suddenly. "You were with the Canfields, were you not?"

"Yes, I—"

"Miss Ashley is Grandmama's goddaughter," Lady Lyndon interjected smoothly.

"Oh, then . . . that is to say . . . how very nice for you, my dear. I had no notion, of course, but if Anne Milbourne is your godmother, I daresay you must be a most unexceptional girl."

"She is." Leah nodded. "I mean to procure a voucher to Almack's for her as soon as I see Sally Jersey."

As they passed on into the ballroom, Caroline could hear Lady Conniston whispering to someone, "Lady Milbourne's goddaughter, you know."

"Buck up, Miss Ashley," Rotherfield encouraged, "for tonight you will be the object of curiosity. 'Twill pass, I can promise you from experience."

Across the floor, Lady Canfield looked up and gasped in shock at the sight of Caroline Ashley on

Rotherfield's arm. "It cannot be! Look at that gown! Juliana, I thought you said she was caring for her godmother!"

Juliana followed her mother's line of vision, and started. "Caro! And Rotherfield!" Her color heightened at his perceived duplicity, and she moved purposefully toward the two of them.

"Juliana!" her mother hissed.

"Nonsense, Mama," she answered in a brittle voice. "Caro is my dearest friend, after all."

But once she reached them, Juliana addressed the earl first, accusing him. "I thought you were my friend, sir!" Then, turning indignantly to Caroline, she added, "And I have been half out of my mind with worry over you!"

"Miss Canfield, I assure you that I have just this evening made Miss Ashley's acquaintance," Rotherfield protested. "Before that, I had no notion that she was staying with Lord and Lady Milbourne or that Leah means to bring her out."

"Bring her out?" Juliana stared.

"Ju, did you not get my letter?" Caroline asked. "I wrote as soon as I arrived at the Milbournes'."

"I have heard nothing since—" She stopped and looked around before lowering her voice to finish, "—since you left with Mr. Bascombe."

"Oh, dear—how everything must look to you then."

"Er . . . I do not believe I would discuss the matter here, were I you," Rotherfield warned. "A more private place, perhaps, would be better. Tell me, Miss Ashley, do you drive out?"

"I have not had the opportunity, my lord."

"Well, then perhaps I may persuade Lady Lyndon to take the both of you up for a turn around the park," he offered. "I should like to hear the tale myself."

"But I wrote to Juliana of it," Caro protested.

"Obviously she did not receive the letter." He cast a meaningful look to where Lady Canfield stood glaring at them.

"Oh." Juliana nodded. "Yes, Mama would not have given it to me, I daresay. But then, she would have had to know, and I do not believe she had the slightest notion, Caro." Turning to Rotherfield, she shook her head. "I should like to go to the park, but Mama would never countenance it, my lord, if she had the least inkling either you or Caro would be there. She dislikes Caro, too, you know."

"You can trust Lady Lyndon to be discreet."

Albert Bascombe had the misfortune to come to Lady Canfield's notice at that moment. His first impulse was to run, but by the time he'd looked around for a place to hide, she was upon him. And, while usually somewhat oblivious of his surroundings, Bertie could tell on the instant that she was less than pleased. Without preamble, she launched into a complete censure of the Earl of Rotherfield's manners, morals, and character that left Bertie bewildered. It was not until she finished that he understood that she meant for him to retrieve his betrothed from the notorious earl's company.

"Me?" He cast a furtive look to where Rotherfield stood, and shook his head. "Uh-unhh. Wouldn't offend him for anything." Just then, Juliana moved a step, and Bertie's attention was arrested by the girl behind her. "Miss Ashley!"

"Yes," sniffed Lady Lenore, " 'tis Miss Ashley, as bold as brass, and looking for the world as though she belongs here. Sick godmother indeed!"

"Uh . . . your pardon, Lady Canfield," Bertie managed while he still stared after Caroline. "Got to find Patrick."

"Patrick? Here? He would not dare!"

"Don't see why not," Bertie insisted loyally. "If Rotherfield can do it, so can Patrick."

"But the scandal—"

"Old story. Ten to one, half the people in this room don't remember precisely what he did even." With that, Bascombe left Lady Canfield standing alone.

He found Patrick lounging against a pillar, his hands

jammed into his coat pockets, his face incredibly bored. The hazel eyes flicked over Bertie, and a wry smile tilted the corners of his mouth.

"Behold the pariah," he said as he indicated the empty area around him.

"Pat, she's here!"

"Ju? Saw her come in with my aunt earlier."

"Miss Ashley—at least I think 'tis Miss Ashley."

Patrick's whole being came alive. "Where?"

"Over there—with Rotherfield and Miss Canfield."

Patrick was unprepared for the rush of emotion he felt when he saw her. A vast feeling of relief and more flooded over him as he stared hard at the transformed Caroline Ashley. He willed her to look his way and was rewarded when she turned her head.

"Pretty thing, ain't she?" Bertie observed.

"Beautiful."

Although some fifty paces separated him from Caro, their eyes met. She paled for an instant and then gave him a tentative little smile. Still stunned, Patrick managed to make his way across the room. In his single-mindedness, he bumped against his aunt.

"You!" Lady Canfield spat at him. "Never say you have a card."

"Bascombe procured one for me."

"Then Lady Conniston cannot be very nice in her tastes," Lady Lenore retorted. "You and Rotherfield! One can only marvel at her thinking!" With that observation, she pushed her way through to Juliana. Giving both Rotherfield and Caroline the cut direct, she addressed her daughter.

"For shame, my dear, but you would ignore your betrothed. I am sure that Mr. Bascombe means to lead you out when the music begins."

"Betrothed?" The earl gave a start, his black eyes suddenly intent. "Am I to wish you happy then, Miss Canfield?"

"Not—"

" 'Twas in the morning paper," Lenore unbent

enough to announce. "And Haverstoke has been most generous to Juliana, since Mr. Bascombe is his heir."

"Mama—"

"Well, 'twill be common knowledge by the end of the evening, anyway, my love. Come—you must not neglect Mr. Bascombe—such an amiable young man."

"Ah, Lady Canfield," Lady Lyndon acknowledged as she joined the group. "I believe you have the acquaintance of Rotherfield, do you not? And, of course, you know Miss Ashley. She has but lately come to live with my grandmother, Lady Milbourne."

"Lady Milbourne," Lenore echoed faintly. "I had no idea."

"Grandmama is Caro's godmother," Leah went on. "And since she has been apprised of Caro's situation, Grandmama is quite determined that she shall be presented."

"Presented? But she has no . . ." Lady Lenore was stunned.

"Expectations? Ah, but she does. There is a small inheritance, I believe."

The interchange between the two women was lost on Caroline, who could only see Patrick. It was as though they were standing apart, just the two of them. In the background, the musicians began playing.

"I went to see your Miss Richards."

Her eyes widened perceptibly. "But—"

"I had to know you were safe."

"Oh." He'd been in her thoughts constantly since she left Calais, and yet it seemed that her memories paled against the man before her. Clad simply in a blue evening coat that would have been austere on anyone else, he presented a picture of manly perfection. Although his expression was sober, his hazel eyes were warm. She colored under his gaze.

"They are playing a waltz, Caroline," he murmured softly. "As I recall, we did not finish the last one we danced."

"Alas, we did not."

"Do you think you have enough credit now to stand up with Westover?"

"Well, I certainly expect to finish what I began," she answered with a smile.

He led her to the floor and slid his arm around her waist before whirling her to the music. For a tall man, he was remarkably graceful and easy to follow. And for once, she was cognizant of the speculative stares around her, and she did not care. She no longer needed to defer to Lady Canfield in constant fear for her livelihood. And certainly if the Milbournes could countenance Rotherfield, they could scarce cavil at Patrick Danvers. Indeed, Lady Anne had said as much.

Bascombe, coerced by Lady Canfield into leading Juliana out, backed into them and almost stumbled. Juliana's smile was frozen on her face, and Bertie looked to be the most miserable man alive despite the envious glances cast his way. It was obvious by the movement of his lips that he counted out the steps like a schoolboy.

"You certainly dance well for one who supposedly has not had much practice," Caroline observed to Patrick as she contrasted him to the hapless Bertie.

"Oh, I've waltzed often enough, Caroline—'twas just not in polite society."

"Then where . . . ?" As soon as the words were out, she wished she could recall them, for it was an impertinence to ask. "Your pardon, I should not have said that."

"No, you should not have." He nodded as he repressed a smile. " 'Tis scarce to my credit, but I never miss the Cyprians' Ball."

"Oh."

"You know, I wish you had not run away," he changed the subject.

"My lord, I could not have gone through with it."

"Patrick," he reminded her.

"Patrick."

"Why did you not contact anyone? Juliana was certain that Bertie'd abandoned you to a fate worse than death."

"I wrote to her as soon as Lord Milbourne and I returned to London."

"She professed to know nothing."

"I can only surmise that Lady Canfield wished to wash her hands of me and threw it away unopened."

"You must tell me how you came to be with the Milbournes, my dear, for I have never been quite so surprised."

Some devil prompted a mischievous gleam in her dark eyes. " 'Tis odd, but that is what Lord Rotherfield said. Indeed, but I am to take a turn in Hyde Park tomorrow to tell him the tale."

"I see." The warmth faded from his expression. "My suit is repugnant, but you will be seen with a man of Rotherfield's stamp. A few new dresses, and now you fancy yourself a countess, I suppose. Well, let me remind you that his reputation is every inch as unsavory as my own." He bit off each word precisely.

"Oh, no! You mistake the matter. I . . ." She stared up in dismay.

"Perhaps I was mistaken in your character, after all."

"And perhaps you are blind!" she snapped with asperity. "I am being presented by Lord and Lady Lyndon, after all, and Lord Rotherfield is a particular friend of the Lyndons. It is a natural curiosity on his part, I am sure—not that I owe you the least explanation, my lord," Caroline added.

"On your high ropes, eh? Well, let me give you one bit of advice, Miss Ashley," Patrick retorted acidly. "Do not be setting your cap for the Earl of Rotherfield, or you'll find yourself in a worse basket than ever. He's head over heels for Leah Barsett!"

"There you are mistaken, sir—I am assured he is not."

Mercifully, the music ended, and Caroline was able to make a dignified exit from the floor. Patrick bowed over her hand, thanked her for the waltz, and moved away. Caroline watched with a heavy heart as he approached Lady Lyndon, and then her attention was claimed by a young exquisite in bottle-green coat and cream trousers whose starched cravat and collar points kept his head firmly facing straight ahead. Reluctantly she agreed to a country dance.

The rest of the evening should have been a triumph for her, but she could scarce remember that no fewer than seven bucks of the *ton* danced with her, or that a very preoccupied Lord Rotherfield took her to supper. To her, it was a failure, since Patrick Danvers had not even remarked her dress or her hair.

16

At the unfashionable hour of three o'clock, Lady Lyndon, professing an interest in going to Hookham's Lending Library, took up Juliana first and then proceeded to Milbourne House for Caroline before going on to meet Lord Rotherfield. Ju and Caro, constrained by Lady Lyndon's presence, occupied the intervening time by discussing the weather, the previous night's ball, Juliana's court presentation, and the Season's matrimonial matches. Both girls stayed away from anything pertaining to Patrick Danvers, Rotherfield, or Albert Bascombe. Leah Barsett leaned back and surveyed them with a mixture of sympathy and amusement.

Rotherfield, always prompt, was waiting with hat and gloves in hand when they arrived. Wearing the somber black he favored, the earl climbed in to take a seat next to Juliana, who had conveniently managed to sit across from the other two ladies.

"Where were you wishful of going, Marcus?" Leah asked.

"Hyde Park. 'Twill be thin of company for another hour or so, so I doubt we shall be much remarked." He settled back against the squabs before turning to Juliana. "Unless, of course, you fear discovery, Miss Canfield?"

"No, of course not."

"Splendid." He looked across at Caroline and nodded. "You are as fine as five-pence, Miss Ashley. You really ought to cultivate that particular shade of green—it becomes you. Madame Cecile's?"

Caroline managed a smile and smoothed the skirt of the gown Lord Westover had bought her before acknowledging the compliment. "Thank you. 'Tis quite my favorite despite all the dresses Lady Milbourne has had made for me. It comes from Calais."

"Calais?" Juliana's brow furrowed in concentration and then lightened as she remembered. "So that was it! Oh, Caro, you've no notion how I puzzled over Mr. Bascombe's letter, I can tell you. None of us could make the least sense of it, but now I can see—it was France, after all!"

"France?" Leah Barsett turned to Caroline. "So you met Grandpapa in France. But how did you come to be there? Grandmama said . . ."

Caroline looked around her for a moment and sighed. "Well, 'tis a long tale, but I daresay if you are to bring me out, you should know of it. Suffice it to say, I was abducted and carried to France in the mistaken notion that I should be grateful to wed someone I considered quite ineligible. I refused, ran away, and found Lord Milbourne, who graciously assisted me with my passage and opened his house to me to prevent my disgrace."

"That's it?" Juliana demanded incredulously. "Caro, it cannot be! If you think that will pass for the whole, you are mistaken. You said it was a long tale."

"I should not like to share the particulars, Ju."

"But we already know you left with Bascombe! And I cannot believe he had enough interest in any female to force a marriage! Indeed . . ." She stopped, her face suddenly arrested for a moment, and then burst out, "Patrick! But he would never—he would not! Caro, never say that Patrick tried to force you into marriage, because I'll not believe it!"

"No, of couse not—he did not know of the scheme

until . . ." Caroline hesitated as she realized that they
were all staring at her curiously.

"Miss Ashley, I can assure you that your concern is
unfounded," Rotherfield broke in. "You are among
friends here."

"Well, I—"

"Do go on, Caroline," Leah urged, "for we have
already surmised much of what must have happened.
You were abducted by Mr. Bascombe and taken to
Calais," she prompted.

Caroline nodded and looked out the window at the
broad tree-lined streets and the well-tended flowerbeds
within the vast expanse of grass. "Well," she answered
finally, " 'tis not nearly so sordid as it must sound, but
Mr. Bascombe asked me to drive with him in this very
park. It was less than a month ago, but it seems to have
been an age." Briefly she sketched the improbable
events of her abduction after Patrick's offer.

"But could you not have stopped him?" Juliana
questioned skeptically. "I mean, from what I know of
Albert Bascombe, I should have thought you could have
outwitted him, Caro."

"Believe me, Ju, I tried." For a moment her dark
eyes met Rotherfield's and she was surprised by the
sudden hostility in them. Thinking it directed somehow
at her, she looked away.

"You refused Danvers'—your pardon, Westover's—
suit?" Rotherfield asked. "I should have thought a
marriage better than Lady Canfield's employ. But then
I suppose that by now I should be accustomed to how
females view reputations. After all, 'twould seem in the
eyes of a lady that one's defending one's honor ought to
be preferable to having numerous liaisons with the
muslin company, but somehow it is not."

"Oh, no! It was not that, precisely." Caroline
thought back to Patrick's first offer and colored
uncomfortably. " 'Twas the reason he offered, sir. I
should not speak of it, but—"

"Ah, the infamous wager."

"You know of it?" She looked up quickly. "Well, then cannot you see that I would not wed simply to give a stranger an heir? I mean, 'tis not very flattering, is it? While I had no fortune, I thought him much the same as a fortune hunter, Lord Rotherfield. To me, it was as though he said, 'Wed me, give me an heir, and I can be rich.' There was certainly no mention of those tender passions necessary to such intimacy."

The hostility in the earl's black eyes faded. "Your pardon, Miss Ashley—I should not have said that. Do go on. You appear to have spirit—could you not have refused passage across?"

"Lord Rotherfield, I made so much mischief for Mr. Bascombe on the way that he drugged me with his mother's sleeping potion. He gave me the worst wine I have ever tasted, but out of thirst, I drank it. Unfortunately, his memory of the dosage was imperfect in the extreme and I count myself fortunate to have survived. I remember nothing of the packet."

"Well, if he cannot read better than he can write, I can believe it," Rotherfield muttered. "I scoured half of London looking for some scrap of information as to your whereabouts."

"You?"

"I asked him, Caro," Juliana explained. "I mean, what was I to do? I couldn't read Bascombe's letter either. I was desperate, so I took the letter before Mama saw it and I told her you'd gone to your sick godmother."

"But you did not even know Lord Rotherfield, Ju."

"That is quite another tale, Miss Ashley," Rotherfield interposed quickly. "So you awoke in Calais then?"

"Yes."

"And?"

"Well, my memory is not precise, as I was ill, but Pat . . . Westover arrived, quarreled with Mr. Bascombe, and then insisted that I must marry him to save my reputation. At first, I thought him in league with Mr. Bascombe, but then realized he was not. Rather than tie either of us in a loveless union, I ran away.''

"And then you met Grandpapa." Leah Barsett leaned to pat Caroline's hand where it worked against the green silk in her lap. "Let us speak no more of what can only distress you. 'Tis over, and now you are free to make a good match of your own choosing.''

Caroline debated whether to tell them the rest, but decided no purpose could be served by bringing up DeVere. She nodded. "You know then what happened after I chanced to meet Lord Milbourne.''

"But I thought Lady Milbourne was your godmother!" Juliana protested. " 'Tis what you said, after all.''

"Well—"

"Since Lady Milbourne's granddaughter is sponsoring her, I see no reason to question it further," Rotherfield interrupted with finality. "Though if I were you, I should discuss his abduction of Miss Ashley with your betrothed. I've half a notion to do so myself.''

"Mr. Bascombe? But I . . . that is—"

Caroline came to Juliana's rescue hastily. "I daresay she has taxed him with it, haven't you, Ju? But I am for Lady Lyndon's suggestion: let us speak no more of this.''

Juliana was torn between a desire to blurt out that Albert Bascombe was the last man in England that she would wed and the knowledge that she would look the veriest fool if she did. Besides, one did not publicly criticize one's mother. Frustrated, she bit back a denial. When she looked up, she was nonplussed to see Rotherfield's black eyes intently watching her. To avoid betraying herself, she turned to the window as though absorbed by the beauty of the park.

"Marcus," Leah asked suddenly, "do you go with us to the Farnsworths' tonight? I daresay 'twill be exceedingly dull, but Grandmama expects Mrs.

Farnsworth to assist with the party we shall be giving Caroline, so there's no help for it—we shall be going.''

"Did I receive a card?"

"If you did not, I can contrive to get one."

"What sort of affair is it?"

"Oh, dear. I knew you would ask," Leah sighed. " 'Tis a musicale—a Mrs. Brentwood will be singing.''

"And we shall be served weak lemonade and stale cake, no doubt," he observed dryly. "Actually, I had thought to accompany Moreson to White's."

"Well, I daresay we can contrive, of course, but I had hoped that you would come so Tony would not have to take two of us. We are just beginning to establish Caro, and . . ."

Caroline was mortified at the blatant lure Leah was casting out on her behalf, but could think of no way to disassociate herself from it without injuring Lady Lyndon's feelings. She too found herself staring determinedly out the window.

If the earl thought it patently odd that he was being called on to establish a lady's reputation rather than destroy it, he concealed his amusement rather well. Besides, the more he knew of Caroline Ashley, the more he was impressed. After all, Lord and Lady Milbourne were well into their seventies and scarcely the sort to attempt to bring any female out. Finally he gave a nod of resignation. "I'll take you up in my carriage about eight, Leah, but I warn you—if this Mrs. Bentwood is a crashing bore, I shall hold you accountable for my headache."

"Done. I am sure we need not stay above an hour or two, Marcus." Leah smiled. "I have never cared much for musicales either, but Caroline must be seen if she is to take."

"Do you go to the Farnsworth thing, Miss Canfield?" Rotherfield suddenly addressed Juliana.

"Yes."

"Good. I shall look forward to seeing you and Mr.

Bascombe there." He noted the stiffness of her posture
and the set of her jaw. "I am certain that Miss Ashley
will contrive to sit with you." He followed her line of
vision out the window and noted the increase in carriage
traffic. "Leah, I think it would be wise to leave before
we are remarked. I should not like to be responsible for
Lady Canfield's reading a peal over the child."

"I am not a child, I am—"

"Betrothed?" the earl supplied helpfully. "And I
know you are eighteen, I believe."

For the first time in her life, Juliana Canfield was at a
loss as to how to deal with a man. Usually, all of them
made cakes of themselves in one way or another within
minutes of being introduced to her, but this one was
different. When his black eyes met hers, she felt a
tremor in her soul, but he gave no indication that he felt
the same. She looked across the seat at Caroline and felt
a stab of jealousy. Leah Barsett and the Milbournes
were going to give Caro every opportunity to be with
Rotherfield while Juliana's mother would see she spent
her time with Bertie Bascombe. And if she were not
careful, she would find herself married to that
paperskull, for she could not depend on his wits to keep
it from happening.

"Marcus . . ." Leah leaned forward to gain his attention. "It grows late, and Juliana's mama will wonder if
we return with no books. Perhaps if you were to escort
Caroline to Grandmama's and come back for us,
'twould be better. She cannot afford to have you go
with us to Hookham's, after all."

Mortified, Caroline hastened to suggest that she go to
the lending library also, but Leah dismissed the notion
in an instant with, "No, that would leave poor Marcus
in the carriage alone, my dear."

"Is your grandfather home, Leah?" Rotherfield
changed the subject abruptly. "I've meant to ask him
about an investment in some of his Indian funds."

"I should think so. Did he say he meant to go out,
Caro?"

"No. He and Lady Milbourne were to meet with his man of business, I believe."

To Juliana, it seemed that Caroline Ashley had joined a conspiracy against her designed to keep her away from the earl. Unfortunately no graceful way to demur came to mind before they reached Hookham's.

After they had set down Leah and Juliana, Caroline and Rotherfield were each lost in solitary thoughts, and conversation lapsed totally. It was not until they found themselves in the Milbourne House drive that either roused to note the other's presence. As the coach rolled to a halt, Rotherfield lifted the window curtain to observe, " 'Twould seem that Milbourne has company, for unless I am mistaken, that is Westover's crest."

Caroline started guiltily and leaned to stare where Rotherfield's hand directed. A flush crept over her cheeks, betraying that Patrick Danvers had been the sole occupant of her thoughts since Hookham's. Rotherfield mistook the heightened color for embarrassment at having to see Lord Westover again, and reached to take her hand reassuringly.

"Miss Ashley, I promise you that you have nothing to fear of him when you are in my company." When she looked up, she was surprised by the sympathy mirrored in the black eyes. "Alas"—he nodded—"my temperament matches his. We are of like reputations, after all."

"But he is not—" She bit back a defense of Patrick Danvers and shook her head. "You are too kind, sir. I could neither expect nor permit you to defend me. Indeed, there is no need."

A faint gleam of amusement lit his eyes at the independent tone of her voice. One black eyebrow shot up skeptically. "No? I should not count on Milbourne's years or Lyndon's temper for protection, Miss Ashley." He turned to step down after the coachman opened the carriage door. Reaching up to her, he lifted her easily and set her on the paving stones. Noting her hesitation when he offered his arm, he urged, "Come—I am going in, anyway."

Patrick Danvers, having taken particular care with his dress and appearance, paused briefly in front of an ornately framed mirror to smooth back an unruly mahogany lock before going out to meet her. As Lord Milbourne's butler had been extremely vague about her whereabouts, Patrick had concluded she probably shopped with Lady Lyndon. The sight of the Lyndon carriage as it drew into the drive seemingly confirmed it.

"Car . . . Miss Ashley." He drew up stiffly as he recognized the tall, dark man beside her, and managed a curt nod. "Your pardon, my lord. I did not expect to see you here."

"Westover." Rotherfield acknowledged him in a voice totally devoid of any warmth.

Caroline dropped her hand from the earl's sleeve and stepped back. To her horror, the two deadliest men in London appeared to be taking each other's measure. The thought that between them they'd killed six men flitted through her mind momentarily. "Lord Westover," she murmured as she stepped between them, "how very kind of you to call." The look she received in return was not kind at all. "Would you perhaps care for a glass of wine?" Her diversion sounded foolish to her own ears.

"I had one while I waited for you."

"Well, then perhaps Lord Rotherfield would take one."

"No."

"Well, I daresay I will have some ratafia." She removed her gloves and walked into the saloon where Patrick had waited. Reaching for the bell pull, she nodded back at the two men. "Would you care to join me, sirs?" For answer, Rotherfield moved to lean against the marble mantel, and Patrick crossed the room to stare through the crosspanes into the side garden. "Well," she ventured brightly as she waited for the footman, "what brings you to Milbourne House, Lord Westover?"

Instead of answering her, Patrick turned to Rotherfield. "Pray excuse us, sir. I would be private with Miss Ashley, if you do not mind."

"But I do mind." Rotherfield straightened his tall frame and surveyed Patrick coldly. "I do not believe Miss Ashley is desirous of furthering your acquaintance, Westover."

" 'Tis not your affair, Marcus!" Patrick flared.

The earl dropped his eyes to study the heavy black-stoned signet ring on his left hand before shrugging. "It is, if I choose to make it so," he answered with deceptive softness.

Caroline watched in disbelief as they appeared to bait each other. Unable to stand it, she turned to Rotherfield. "Please, sir, 'tis quite all right. I do not mind seeing Lord Westover alone for a few minutes." When Rotherfield did not look at her, she touched his sleeve tentatively. "I believe Lord Milbourne to be in the library, sir—'tis his custom to spend his afternoons there when he does not go out."

"Very well, but I shall leave the door open if you should need assistance, Miss Ashley." His eyes met Patrick's over her head. "I give you five minutes, Westover."

"Five minutes?" Patrick moved to her side. " 'Tis not even his house! The incredible arrogance of the man! I ought—"

"Why are you here?" she cut in quickly.

"Your delight in my presence overwhelms me," he murmured sarcastically. "Actually, Caroline, I came to apologize for my lamentable manners last night. I thought that we could take a turn about the park at the fashionable hour, if you did not mind too much."

"Do you really think I would get into a carriage with you, my lord?"

"Patrick. And I take leave to tell you, Caroline, that you are far safer with me than with Rotherfield. At least, my duels were fought for principles; his were fought for women."

"Lord Rotherfield's behavior has been correct in the extreme, Patrick," she retorted stiffly. "And I fail to see what concern it is of yours. Lady Lyndon—"

"Leah Barsett is blind where he is concerned! And she is a married lady—she can survive the association as long as Tony Barsett does not cut up a dust! You, on the other hand, cannot! His reputation—"

"Is no worse than yours!" she shot back.

"He's a bloody blackguard!"

"He is not!"

"Do not be a fool, Caroline—Rotherfield is worse than I ever thought of being."

"At least he is received! You will find him at *ton* parties—which cannot be said of you!" She saw him blanch and wished she could call back the words. "Your pardon, Patrick—I should not have said that." To her dismay, he reached to pick up his hat. "I only meant that—"

"You only meant that I am a coward," he finished for her. "I have cared little enough what a pack of fops and dandies thought of me, but I can see that it matters to you. Well, Miss Ashley, you can expect to see me at everything—if only to prove it can be done. Good day, Miss Ashley."

"My lord, please—"

"No—you have made it perfectly plain that my suit is hopeless." He jammed his hat on his head and walked through the open door.

She stood rooted in place for a moment, and then ran after him. "Patrick, wait! I did not mean—"

The door slammed in her face.

Tears of frustration brimmed. Behind her, Rotherfield came out of Lord Milbourne's library. His eyes traveled to the door that had closed with such force and then back to her face. "I am sorry, my dear. I should not have left you alone with him, after all. He's overset you needlessly."

"No—no—I am quite all right, sir. But if you will but

excuse me . . ." She clapped her hand over her mouth to stifle a moan and ran up the stairs to hide her misery. Sobbing, she flung herself on her bed and gave vent to a healthy bout of tears.

17

Mrs. Farnsworth, an indomitable hostess who firmly believed that the ensuing gossip often made the event, greeted the arrival first of Rotherfield and his party and later Lord Westover with remarkable equanimity. Certainly, with Brummell, the Prince Regent, Lords Ponsonby, Alvanley, Grahame, Haverstoke, and a host of other leaders of the *ton* present, she knew her little affair would not go unremarked. But with Rotherfield, the Lyndons, and Westover—well, she could expect to hear of it for days. With an air of total self-satisfaction, she smiled indulgently as Albert Bascombe followed his betrothed down the receiving line.

"Don't know Beethoven from that other fellow," Bertie muttered under his breath. "Don't know why m'father made me come. Don't want to do the pretty by you—don't."

"Mozart," Juliana hissed. "And I do not know why you are come either. I'd as lief you'd stayed home, believe me."

Shocked by this unloverlike display by the *ton*'s newest engaged couple, Mrs. Farnsworth raised her glass and squinted at them. "In my day, young man," she addressed Bertie, "a fellow didn't complain until after the wedding! Humph!"

"Ain't complaining—ain't musical, that's all," Bertie defended.

"Mr. Bascombe," Juliana whispered as they left the line, "have you seen Caro?"

"Miss Ashley? How could I? You was with me. If I'd seen her, you would have also."

Juliana sighed. It was going to be an interminable evening if she did not find someone to converse with. It was uncomfortable enough receiving the good wishes of a totally mystified *ton* without having to endure her unwanted betrothed. And while she resented even pretending to accept the betrothal, it galled her that Bascombe did not even bother with the appearance of caring a fig about her. She looked up to see that he was already several steps ahead of her and she had to catch up. Smiling at a fat matron who appeared surprised by Bascombe's attitude, Juliana clasped Bertie's arm determinedly and gave him a pinch.

"Ouch! Why'd you do that?" he blurted out. "How would you like it if I was to—"

"Be quiet!" Juliana ordered.

"But—";

Dragging him out of anyone's hearing, Juliana hissed at him, "You might at least appear to be pleased when someone congratulates you, Mr. Bascombe. Before you bumbled into Mama's clutches, I was considered a highly desirable female, you know."

"Then cry off," he told her bluntly.

"I cannot—Mama would bury me at Crosslands. I'd never get another Season."

"Hang your mama!" Bertie looked across to where Lady Canfield stood conversing with his father. "I got other worries, Miss Canfield. If you don't do something, m'father's going to have us leg-shackled in a trice. 'Take her to Italy on your wedding trip,' he says!"

"I would not go as far as Cheapside with you!"

"Then cry off."

"Bascombe!"

To Bertie's horror, Lord Rotherfield was bearing down on them. He took in the earl's austere dress and his coldly handsome face, and a chill ran down his spine. They could talk of Patrick, but Bertie'd not want to quarrel with Rotherfield either. He put a hand where Juliana's rested on his arm, a gesture more designed to give him security than to protect her. Amazed, he saw his betrothed change from a carping harridan to a reigning Incomparable.

"R-Rotherfield," Bertie stammered.

"Allow me to wish you happy, sir."

Bertie goggled when he perceived that the earl was regarding him almost pleasantly. "I say, deuced nice of you, my lord!"

"The attachment is of long standing, I presume?"

"Eh? Uh . . . no, not precisely." Bertie felt Juliana's fingers tighten on his sleeve. "Sort of hasty, actually. Met her one week—popped the question the next, I guess you could say."

"With a trip to France in between." The black eyebrow rose as the earl surveyed the squirming Bertie. "How very busy you've been, old fellow." A faint smile curved the corners of his mouth.

"Eh? France? Uh . . ."

"You are very fortunate to have come about so quickly."

"Have you heard Mrs. Bentwood sing, my lord?" Juliana asked to divert Rotherfield.

"Alas, I have not, but I daresay I shall endure it." The smile faded. "Your pardon, Bascombe, but I seem to have misplaced Miss Ashley in this squeeze. Perhaps you would allow Miss Canfield to assist in finding her?"

"Eh? Oh, be glad to!"

Elated despite the glare her mother cast her, Juliana took Rotherfield's arm. His next words sent her spirits crashing down. "You must have wanted to be a countess very badly, Miss Canfield, if you can stomach Bertie Bascombe. Or were you looking for a rich but amiable fool?"

"Wha—" She stiffened in outrage. "How dare you, sir?"

"Haverstoke's in remarkably good health and scarce out of his prime. No, if you fancied yourself a countess, you should have tried less chancy waters. His father could well outlive him."

"I do not see this as any of your business, sir!"

"No? I could have sworn you were casting out lures to me, child. But then perhaps you considered Bertie Bascombe more of a certainty."

"Of all the things to say!" she gasped indignantly.

"Ju! Have you seen Caro?" Patrick drew up short when he realized she was with Rotherfield.

"No, but it is all of a piece!" she snapped in asperity. "Everyone seems to be looking for dear Caro, after all. If you will excuse me, Lord Rotherfield, I really must be getting back to Albert before Mama cuts up a dust."

"Lud!" Patrick looked heavenward when she left. "What freak of distemper ails her?"

"The price of a rich title, most likely," the earl muttered after her. In that instant, he made up his mind on something that he had been toying with since Juliana's betrothal became known. Turning back to Patrick, he warned, "I should not bother Miss Ashley, were I you, Westover. She finds your attentions offensive."

"That is none of your affair."

"I mean to make it mine." The earl's black eyes stared into Patrick's hazel ones. "She prefers me to you."

"I should not want to quarrel with you, Marcus, but I am not afraid of you," Patrick reminded him stiffly.

"It may come to that, but I hope not." Rotherfield reached to draw out an onyx-lidded snuffbox. Flicking it open expertly, he extended it to Patrick. "Excellent sort—had it from Petersham's best mix."

"No, I dislike sneezing." Patrick counted silently to hold his temper in check. Looking across the room to where Leah Barsett stood chatting with her husband and their hostess, he shook his head. "I thought you were head over heels for Lady Lyndon."

"The fair Leah? No. There was a time when I thought so, but then I realized my case was hopeless. I owe her my thanks, however—had it not been for her friendship, I should never have ventured back into the *ton*."

"It surprised me that Anthony Barsett never ran you through."

"The fiery Tony? Oh, we were to meet once, but then he realized 'twas nonsense. She loved him, after all. And I was no fool—I knew it."

"So now you want Caro. Tell me, Marcus, who will it be next year? Or the year after?"

"Despite what you think, I am a man of honor."

Patrick stopped. Those had been almost his very words to Caroline Ashley once. Rotherfield flicked the case closed without taking a pinch. Returning it to his pocket, he executed a stiff bow to Patrick and moved away.

The candles were being systematically doused to dim the room and still Patrick had not found Caroline. He made one last sweep of the room before reluctantly taking a seat. The matchmaking mama next to him gave him a broad smile until she placed his handsome face with his notorious name. The smile turned to a glare as she made her daughter move over another chair.

"I say, Miss Ashley," Bertie whispered desperately behind a wall of potted palms, "you've got to help me! If something ain't done, I'm going to be tied to Miss Canfield forever!"

"They cannot make you do it, Mr. Bascombe. I daresay if you go to Lord Haverstoke and explain—"

"No." He shook his head morosely. "He thinks its a capital idea. Lud! I'd rather marry you than her."

In spite of the abduction and everything else, Caroline felt a certain amount of sympathy for Bertie's plight. After having listened to how it had come out, she could see the entire scene in her mind, and she knew exactly how Lenore Canfield had coerced him. "I don't see what I can do about it," she mused slowly. "Perhaps Westover can think of something."

"Patrick?" Bertie scoffed. "Un-uhhh—got his own problems just now, what with the wager and his Uncle Vernon's will and all that. Time's running out, you know."

"I'd almost forgotten." Suddenly she was struck by inspiration. "Mr. Bascombe, have you spoken with Juliana's father?"

"Un-uhhh."

"Sir Max is quite the dearest person. Indeed, one can scarcely fathom that he married Lady Lenore, once one knows him. Anyway, perhaps you could tell him that you never actually offered for Juliana. I am sure he would not expect you to wed with her if your feelings were not truly engaged."

"Well, they ain't."

"Tell him."

"Can't—he's gone to Somerset or someplace."

"Well, tell him when he gets back. No one would expect you to marry her without her father being there."

"Hadn't thought of that," Bertie breathed in relief. "You know, Miss Ashley, you are a very good sort of girl—for a female, I mean."

"Thank you, Mr. Bascombe. But I believe we shall be left in darkness if we do not find seats. Unless I am mistaken, it appears that Lady Canfield is holding a chair for you."

"Un-uhhh. Going to sit with you—you ain't trying to marry me," he insisted.

The room was crowded with people milling about for seats. Caroline did not see the Barsetts or Rotherfield. Unconsciously she scanned the room for Patrick, and then saw him seated next to a woman and her daughter. Well, what could she expect? she chided herself as her spirits sank. He had to have a wife, after all, or he would lose his fortune. She finally spied half a row of unoccupied chairs in the back. "Come on then," she whispered to Bertie, "else we shall be left standing."

Mercifully, Mrs. Bentwood proved to be a competent songstress with a rich soprano voice. And, unlike some singers Caro had heard, she had some expression to her delivery. From time to time, Caroline glanced over to her companion, who sat in dismal silence even when the rest of the audience broke into applause. Poor Bertie, she thought. His poor brain was no match for the schemes of a Lenore Canfield. And he was right: married to Juliana, he could expect to spend a life of misery, for Caro was certain that the high-spirited girl would come to disgrace. No, Juliana needed a strong person like Patrick—or Rotherfield.

As the candles were relit after the program, Caroline rose to find that Patrick Danvers had made his way over to her. She turned around and collided with him, righting herself by clutching at his arms. "Jade!" he hissed as he set her in front of him.

"What?" She stared, stunned.

"Don't come the innocent with me, Caro!"

"My lord, I have not the slightest notion of what—"

"You know very well! I cannot believe I was so mistaken in your character!"

Caroline looked around her and was mortified to see that they had attracted a small crowd of extremely interested spectators. "Please, my lord—"

"Patrick," he bit off precisely.

"Very well—Patrick. I would prefer not to discuss whatever this is in public. I—"

Before she could finish her sentence, he'd grasped her elbow and was propelling her toward the French doors that had been opened to cool the room. Wordlessly he steered her out into the fragrant garden behind the Farnsworth house. As soon as they reached a dark path, he stopped and turned her around.

"Just what do you think you are doing? I shall be

quite ruined—you cannot just drag me out here without—'' Her words were muffled as he pulled her into his arms and bent his head to hers. She barely had time to close her eyes before she felt the strong, warm pressure of his lips. For an instant she gave herself up to the heady feel of being held by him, and then she began to struggle. Abruptly he released her. His hazel eyes glittered in the faint moonlight. "Does Rotherfield do that for you?'' he rasped.

"You . . . you beast!'' she choked. "How dare you!'' She pulled away and stumbled back down the path while he stared after her. Tripping over a low bench, she literally fell into the Earl of Rotherfield's arms.

"Are you all right, Miss Ashley?''

"Yes . . . no . . . ooooh!'' Angry tears welled in her eyes, but she made no move to brush them away. Rotherfield put an arm around her shoulders and started her back to the house.

"You know that you cannot go back in like this, don't you? Full half the place saw you come out with Westover, and the other half saw me come after you.'' He stopped and took out his handkerchief. "Blow your nose, Miss Ashley,'' he ordered brusquely, "and calm yourself. The tabbies are going to have a bowl of cream over this, no matter what, but I mean to spike their guns as best I can.''

Nodding, she blew and then dabbed at her eyes with a dry corner of the linen square. "I . . . I am fine—angry, but that's all.''

"Good.''

When they walked back in, there were countless curious stares and a buzz of comments spread over the room. Behind them, a furious Patrick Danvers came through the double French doors. Caroline saw Lenore Canfield's smug expression and the shock on the hostess's face. Rotherfield stopped and calmly picked an errant leaf out of Caro's hair before taking her hand. Moving directly to Mrs. Farnsworth, he announced baldly, "Wish me happy, for Miss Ashley is to be my countess." The room spun around Caroline as she stared in helpless disbelief. The buzz turned into a roar. She closed her eyes for a moment and when she opened them, she could see a white-faced Patrick Danvers turn and walk out. She opened her mouth to disclaim the betrothal and then shut it, realizing that she could not publicly embarrass the earl for his kindness.

18

Caroline awoke after an extremely restless night hoping that somehow she had only dreamed the bizarre events of Mrs. Farnsworth's party. All night long, she had been tormented by Patrick Danvers' kiss and Rotherfield's enigmatic smile. As she dawdled over her morning chocolate, she relived again every preposterous moment in the garden and saw anew the look of shocked disbelief written on all those faces when the earl had announced his betrothal. It was ludicrous in the extreme to find that she had gone from being a totally ineligible female to being pursued by two of the most notorious men in the country. Had she read her story in one of the romances at Hookham's, she would have dismissed it as utterly ridiculous.

Countess of Rotherfield. The image of the earl floated before her for a moment—cold, austere, mocking. Why had he done it? Kindness? To pique Patrick Danvers? As much as she could remember, there'd never been any *on-dits* about a quarrel between the two men. Did he think himself taken with her? Somehow, as Caroline reviewed every word of conversation they'd exchanged, she did not think so. What could possibly have prompted him to take such a rash step?

Mrs. Farnsworth's look of stunned confusion floated before her. Caro'd almost blurted out that it wasn't so—that he'd not offered and she'd not accepted—but there was such fury in Lady Canfield's expression that she'd said nothing. And in doing so, she'd made the fiction fact. Rotherfield. She had no more desire to wed with him than with Patrick Danvers. Not true, she admitted to herself. She had less desire to be wed to him, for she knew now that it was Patrick she wanted. Well, she'd certainly shut that door once and for all. Not even Patrick would pursue someone else's betrothed. With that lowering thought, she pushed away her tray and swung her legs over the side of the bed.

Lady Milbourne's dresser, Marsh, entered the room and laid out a demurely cut rose muslin gown, drawers, petticoat, and zona without intruding on Caroline's thoughts. Usually condescending in her attitude, she now stood back respectfully and waited.

"Oh, thank you, Marsh," Caro murmured absently without rising.

"Would you be wanting your hair done this morning, miss?"

"Thank you, but I can brush it myself."

"Your pardon, Miss Ashley, but you'll be wanting to be in particular looks, I should think."

"Why?"

"Well, there is Lady Lyndon already arrived below, and with Lord Milbourne. I believe she means to take you out."

"It must be a mistake—there were no plans—"

"Ah, there you are, my love!" Leah Barsett breezed into the room like a soft blue cloud. "Your pardon for intruding before you are about, but we really must be out early. I sent a note round to Cecile's and she will measure you if we can contrive to be there before her regular appointments."

"Measure me?" Caro echoed faintly. "But I cannot afford—"

"Nonsense. Rotherfield has already assured me he means to pay for your trousseau, my dear. It would not do for the Countess of Rotherfield to go about in dresses made anywhere but Madame's, after all." Leah stood back and surveyed Caro's disheveled state with a smile. "My dear Caro, your days of practicing shocking economies are over."

"I cannot let the earl pay for my clothes, Lady Lyndon."

"Leah. And he is not merely 'the earl' to you now, is he? He is your betrothed." Leah Barsett walked over and picked up the blue muslin. "Charming, but nothing like what you will become used to. Marcus is extremely wealthy, Caro. Here—let Marsh help you, and I will go down and wait for him."

"Rotherfield? Here?" Somehow, Caroline did not think she could face him after the previous night.

"But of course. Marcus has the most impeccable taste."

Caroline dressed hurriedly after Leah left. Perhaps she would have the opportunity to tell the earl that she did not expect him to go through with his scheme, that she was grateful, but she could not allow him to sacrifice so much. Even as she thought it, she realized how ridiculous she would sound, for Rotherfield was a man, after all, and men had the most idiotish notions of honor. Patrick Danvers had proven that to her.

Unused to the ministrations of servants, Caroline picked up her nightrail and hung it neatly in the wardrobe. Her eye caught a glimpse of the green silk dress, and she wanted to cry.

By the time she made it downstairs, Rotherfield was already there. He looked up from where he conversed with Milbourne and smiled at her. Somehow, he did not appear quite as forbidding as he had in her tormented dreams.

"Charming, my dear," he approved as he took in her new blue muslin dress. "We have not much time, as I am promised to my man of affairs this afternoon. I was just consulting with Lord Milbourne about what you will require, and I believe we have come to terms that will please you.''

"Uh . . ." For an instant, she wanted to tell them all that she could not do it, but then she saw Leah and Milbourne beaming at her.

"Marcus will settle fifteen thousand on you, my dear, and allow you five hundred pounds each quarter," the frail Milbourne told her with the air of one infinitely satisfied with the arrangement. "Once the heir is born, there will be an additional five thousand pounds."

But Caroline was not attending the particulars, as she was still trying to assimilate the first fifteen thousand. "Fifteen." She nodded slowly.

" 'Tis most generous, Caro," Leah reminded her.

"I took the liberty of bringing my mother's ring," the earl cut in as he extended a small box. " 'Tis a ruby, but if you prefer another stone, we can stop at Hamlet's in Cranbourne Alley." When she made no move to take the box, he opened the lid himself and took out a ring with a blood-red center stone the size of a bird's egg. Reaching for her hand, he slipped the ruby ring on her finger and tried it against the knuckle. "I do not believe you'll lose it," he decided.

She stared down at the symbol of an unwanted betrothal. "It's . . . it's very nice," she told him finally.

"Good. I have sent the notices in to the *Gazette* and the *Morning Chronicle*, so you need have no fear of any unpleasant gossip concerning Westover. Now, if you do not mind too much, we'd best be going. I thought to go to Tattersall's later in hopes of finding you a mare. You do ride, do you not, Miss Ashley?"

"Yes, of course."

"Then we shall begin being seen mornings in the park. The sooner the *ton* gets used to seeing us, the less gossip there will be. I am a firm believer in confronting mine enemies whenever possible. They do not like it, but they back away. Perhaps you would care to go to the theater tonight to see Kean in *Richard III*? Or would you prefer the ballet or opera? I believe Catalini is in *Figaro* and Vestris is dancing in Covent Garden."

"But of course she will wish to see Kean! Tony and I were planning to attend, after all, and we shall be a party," Leah decided for them. " 'Twill be vastly diverting, for I know all London cannot wait to see dear Caro."

"And do you have the wedding trip planned also?" Rotherfield responded dryly.

"That, Marcus, I leave to you," Leah answered, unabashed.

"My lord, may I be private with you for an instant?" Caroline cut in desperately, "I—"

"But of course, my dear. If Leah and Lord Milbourne will pardon us, we can step into one of the saloons."

Lady Lyndon frowned, but said nothing. Caroline led the way to the smaller, private parlor situated at the back of the house, and waited while the earl shut the door behind them. Her palms were damp and her mouth dry as she tried to think of words to thank him for his kindness while making it plain she could not wed him. When he turned back to face her, his eyes met hers and seemed to read her thoughts. A faint smile lifted one corner of his mouth, and he nodded.

"You think we should not suit," he noted matter-of-factly, "but you are wrong, I believe. You behold in me a man much disappointed in love, a man who has made a fool of himself more than once for a pretty face, so I am not like to come into a marriage with foolish expectations, Caroline."

"My lord—"

"And I suspect that your own heart is not unbruised, my dear," he continued, "which is precisely why we should suit. I am nearing thirty and I am the last of my line, Caroline. My salad days are over and I am ready to settle down respectably. My eyes tell me you are a very lovely lady, my mind tells me you are a female of character, and my heart tells me that I can make you content." He moved closer and reached to touch her shoulders. "The burning passion you yearn for burns itself out, consumed by the very fire that first feeds it—believe me, none knows that better than I. In the end, it is regard that matters, and I am certain we can have that. Let Westover win his wager with another— wed with me and save us both from the folly of foolish passion. I can offer you wealth—more than you can dream—and I can set you above those who once ignored you."

"But I don't love you!" she wrung out hopelessly.

"Love?" His mouth curved sardonically and his black eyes betrayed bitterness. "Love is an illusion, my dear—I know. Do not let me make a fool of myself yet again. Save me from repeating the follies of my youth." He bent his head to brush his lips against hers. "Wed with me, Caroline, and save me from myself."

It was as though she felt the pain that lay beneath the carefully controlled facade he presented to the *ton*. The image of Patrick Danvers as last she'd seen him flitted briefly through her brain, telling her anew that she'd lost him. Rotherfield's eyes, black and intent, promised her a life of safety and security. Slowly she dropped her gaze and nodded. "All right, my lord."

"We shall establish and redeem each other, Caroline," he promised.

19

Being the center of attention, both friendly and unfriendly, was a novel experience for the plain Miss Ashley from Miss Richards' school, but she managed to quell her ever-rising panic and meet the *ton* headlong. From time to time in the next couple of weeks, she saw Patrick Danvers at functions, but he made no particular effort to cross her path. She found herself in the ignominious position of being center-stage while he drifted off in the wings, so to speak. But at least, she noted with diminishing satisfaction, he had kept his word: he was attending various affairs despite the censure of his peers. And she was hearing less and less indignant gossip about him.

But Juliana—Caroline was mystified about the girl's behavior. She had expected Lady Canfield to be spiteful and vicious, but she was unprepared for the sudden coldness of her former charge. Had it not been for the hapless Bertie, forced by his father to squire his beautiful betrothed about, Caroline would have had no discourse with Juliana at all. As it was, Bertie fairly pulled the girl over to see her during intermission at the opera one night.

"Miss Ashley!" Bertie took in Caro's new deep green gown and nodded. "Ought to wear green all the time—ain't that so, Miss Canfield?"

Caroline had to suppress a smile at the way Bertie stubbornly insisted on formal address with his betrothed. "Thank you, sir. Hello, Juliana."

She recognized the mulish set of the jaw as the girl turned her attention to her. "Miss Ashley."

Rotherfield started to say something to Juliana and then thought better of it. Instead, he bowed slightly to Caroline and murmured, "I believe I see Bennington over there, my dear. If you do not object, I shall pay a call whilst your friends are here."

As soon as the earl was out of hearing, Bertie shook his head. "Devilish handsome fellow, but cold, if you was to ask me. Don't know what you was thinking of to take him instead of Patrick."

"It is as plain as a pikestaff," Juliana sniffed. "Our little Caro plotted the whole thing, I'll wager. She saw a chance to be a countess, and she maneuvered Rotherfield into offering for her."

Caroline stared, unable to credit the venom in Juliana's voice. "Ju—"

"Don't speak to me, you viper!" the younger girl snapped. Her cornflower-blue eyes met Caroline's for an instant, and then her face crumpled. "Oh, Caro, how could you?" she wailed miserably. Covering her mouth with her gloved hand, she turned precipitately and ran from Rotherfield's box.

"Got to go, Miss Ashley," Bertie murmured apologetically. "Don't know what queer notion she's got now. Me—I wish you happy—just wish it was Patrick, that's all. But she's been in a devilish poor way ever since you got engaged."

"Perhaps she just needs to rest."

"Well, Lady Canfield ain't going to hear of it. I need the rest, I can tell you, but between her and m'father, I ain't going to get any. Don't know why m'father likes Juliana's mama, either, because the only way he's going to make her happy is to pop off early," Bertie announced with disgust. "Well," he sighed as he watched his betrothed being ogled by a fellow from the pit, "no help for it, I suppose. Got to go after her."

Disturbed by Juliana's outburst, Caroline sank back in her seat and tried to make sense of it. It was obvious that the girl and Albert Bascombe were horribly mismatched, for the high-spirited Juliana could never be happy with a man she could rule. No, Juliana needed someone strong—someone like Patrick . . . or Rotherfield. Caroline looked across to where the earl lounged in Bennington's box and saw him watching Juliana and Bertie. It was a revelation—she'd seen that look once before when Patrick Danvers heard Rotherfield announce her own betrothal. There'd been a terrible mix-up—Rotherfield wanted Juliana.

She felt like an outsider, an intruder, watching the earl. Studiously she turned her head away from him and scanned the boxes to her left. With a jolt that struck painfully at her own heart, she saw Patrick with a woman she did not know. At first, she thought it was a member of the muslin company, but then she watched carefully. The awful conviction that the lady was Quality made her almost ill. Patrick said something amusing and the woman laughed.

"Bascombe gone?" Rotherfield asked as he rejoined her. When she did not answer, his black eyes followed where she looked. " 'Twould seem Westover is making a push in that quarter," he observed quietly.

"Yes."

"I daresay he has to, if he is to have even the slightest chance at the Danvers Fortune."

Caroline turned around, suddenly aware that the black eyes were intent on her. "I suppose so," she managed noncommittally.

Abruptly he reached for her hand and fingered the blood-ruby ring. "Would you like to go to Oakland? We could be married by special license there, and we'd never have to see them again."

It came to her suddenly that he was an immensely

proud man despite the cuts of the *ton*, and that he meant to marry her before Juliana wed Bertie. It was a devil of a coil for him, for her, and for all of them. "Oakland?"

"My home. It is an enormous rock barn built in Tudor times. The original manor belonged to the Bishop of Durham, but was confiscated by Henry."

"Sir, I believe plain speaking would serve us best." She sucked in her breath and let it out slowly as one is wont to do when faced with an unpleasant task. "I believe that you are more than half in love with Juliana."

He was silent for a moment, and then he spoke carefully. "Caroline, I am nine-and-twenty—soon to be thirty, in fact. She is a foolish, headstrong chit bent on destruction, and she is but eighteen. And regardless of the reason she became engaged to the slowtop, her family is determined to see the marriage."

"But they despise each other!"

"Miss Ashley . . ." His black eyes met hers and he continued in patient resignation. "I told you once that I am unwilling to make a fool of myself again."

"But if you care for her—"

"Moon madness," he dismissed. "And even if it were not, there is still the matter of her family."

"Lenore Canfield is a viper!" she announced with feeling.

He sighed heavily and leaned forward to stare at the railing before him. "You cannot have known the story, else you'd know why I cannot go against her parents."

"My lord, regardless of what happened years ago, you deserve your happiness! You punish yourself too harshly, I think."

"It is not a pretty tale," he began in a low, measured voice, "but if we are to wed, perhaps you should know of it." He drew in a deep breath and exhaled slowly before continuing. "I was barely nineteen—scarce into my salad days even—when I fell passionately in love with a woman I shall not name. She was older than I by some six years and bored with an elderly husband's complaints. Suffice it to say that we eloped together— fled first to a property I hold in Ireland, and then when we could no longer stay there, on to the Continent despite Boney's threat. She bore a child that did not survive." He stared unseeing, unaware that the lights were being doused again. "My guardians cut off the money, and she found a wealthier man in Guelph. One day, I awoke to find her gone. I followed her and fought her lover, but it did not end. Within the month, she'd found another. I could see then that there'd be no end to it, and I let her go. When I returned to England, her brother called me out. He was scarce older than I, but I killed him when we met beyond Smithfield. It was not pretty—he lingered some weeks, Caroline, and then he died. I fled to Spain."

"My lord, you must not—"

"Strangely enough, I met one of Elizabeth's other lovers there—a soldier in the Tenth Hussars—and he told me the child she bore was his. I suppose I must have looked the richer fool to fleece."

By now, the lights were out and the orchestra had begun to play. The earl straightened up slowly and leaned back in his chair. "We dueled, of course, and he lies there still. Three men dead for my foolish passion. No, I'd not make the same mistake again."

"You were but a boy! You cannot have known what she was! But Juliana—"

"No. We are far safer, you and I, with each other. You have spirit, but you are not unkind; you have beauty, but you are not obsessed with it; and you are intelligent. Passions fade, Caroline, but regard does not," he repeated in much the same vein as he had before. "I would not fly in the face of the Canfields to possess a girl certain to lead me to destruction again."

"You mistake the matter then, my lord, for Juliana is high-spirited, yes, but she is good-hearted."

"Tell Albert Bascombe that—not me."

The tenor began to sing, making further conversation not only impolite but also difficult. Caroline sat beside the earl and pondered what she ought to do. Certainly she could not cry off—not after what he'd endured. But neither could she marry him knowing that he wanted Juliana. She strained her eyes in the darkened opera house for a glimpse of Viscount Westover and was disappointed. Finally Rotherfield leaned so close their shoulders brushed and murmured, "The lady is Anthea Lyddesdale, my dear—a widow of exemplary reputation."

"Who?"

"The one sitting with Westover."

Her eyes widened at the sympathy in his voice. Unable to reply, she stared miserably at her folded hands and saw the faint glitter of Rotherfield's ruby on her finger.

20

The library was in darkness except for a single candle that flickered on the carved marble mantelpiece. Crump pushed the door open and peered within anxiously, his eyes following the wedge of light cast from the chandelier in the hallway.

"Milford?"

He said it softly, tentatively, while hesitating from the safe distance of the doorway. A lone figure sitting slumped back in a leather wing chair before the empty fireplace stirred slightly but did not turn around.

"Aye."

"I brought you some food."

"Crump . . ." Patrick's voice was slurred slightly as he lurched to his feet. "A man does not want food when he is in his cups. Wine—bring me some more wine."

"But, my lord—"

"Aye, I'm foxed." Patrick moved unsteadily to the table and held up a bottle. "Never mind, Crump—thersh more here."

The butler's attention was suddenly diverted by the sound of the huge brass knocker on the front door. With the tray of food still in his hand, Crump backed out to answer it. Relief flooded his face as he admitted Albert Bascombe.

"Hallo, Crump—Patrick in?"

"Aye, and in the devil's own temper, he is—won't eat, won't bathe, and won't stir from his library! Mayhap you can reason with him!"

"Me? Un-uhhh—if he's in a taking, I'll come back."

"Master Bascombe," the butler fixed Bertie with an icy stare and demanded, "if you were overset, would he leave you be?"

"No." Bertie hesitated for a moment and then capitulated. "All right, I'll see to him."

He found Patrick leaning back in the chair, his long legs crossed and resting on the empty metal grate in the fireplace. A near-empty wine glass sat precariously on his chest, bearing testimony to the fact that he was all but disguised with drink. While Bertie watched, Patrick raised the glass to contemplate the dregs, then drained it and consigned it to shatter against the fire bricks.

"Damn!" he muttered in frustration. "She cannot prefer him to me—I at least have some fire! The man's cold as ice!"

"Who?" Bertie asked without thinking. "Oh, I collect you mean Rotherfield, don't you? Shouldn't think that, Pat—I mean, the fellow's been in a deuced lot of trouble over women, ain't he?"

Patrick looked up at the sound of Bertie's voice, casting such a baleful glance that Bertie recoiled. "I said he was cold as ice," Patrick repeated awfully.

"Well, I ain't a female, of course," Bertie hastened to add. "Don't know what she sees in him, either."

Uncrossing his feet, Patrick kicked the grate forcefully, and came out of his chair. For the briefest instant he swayed slightly and then maintained his balance. "He's damned handsome—devilish handsome —that's what it is," he pronounced with authority. "Don't matter that he's cold! She can sit around looking at him!" He moved to tower over Bertie, shouting, "Deny it! He's a damned handsome fellow!"

"Well—"

"You cannot—can you?" Patrick turned away, muttering, "Well, neither can I . . . neither can I. Damn him! Damn her!"

It had been a long time since Bertie could remember Patrick being in such a taking. Not even when goaded into a duel had Patrick displayed such temper. Bertie tried to touch his shoulder, only to be shaken off. "I say, Pat," he asked in alarm, "you ain't thinking of meeting him—you ain't, are you?"

"No! That's the devil of it, Bertie! I cannot call him out even! 'Tis no matter of honor, and if I did, the clubs would be full of gossip about her! I should look the veriest fool and she would be ruined." He ran his fingers through his thick dark red hair in distraction.

"The clubs are full of gossip anyway, Pat," Bertie reminded him. "I mean, what with you dangling after Mrs. Lyddesdale, there's betting everywhere that you'll win the Danvers fortune. It ain't all bad, neither," he consoled, " 'cause the odds are tipping in your favor."

Instead of mollifying the viscount, this news seemed to enrage him further. "They are betting I can win Anthea Lyddesdale?" he demanded in strangled accents. "I cannot even be seen in the company of a respectable female without ruining her reputation! Crump!"

"My lord?" the butler responded from the safety of the door.

"Order my bath!" Patrick rubbed the stubble on his chin and growled, "I need a bath, a shave, and evening clothes." Turning back to the perplexed Albert Bascombe, he snapped, "Where is the wagering the heaviest?"

"I don't know . . . uh . . . White's, I think, but—"

"I mean to go there then."

Bertie stared. Patrick's anger had cleared his bleary-eyed look and replaced it with one of steely determination. Shuddering involuntarily, Bertie protested, "But, Pat—"

"Just because my life is ruined is no reason to allow the slander of an innocent female!"

"But—"

"Bertie, I mean to call a halt to this nonsense—I am paying Charlie off," Patrick flung over his shoulder as he left the room.

It took a few moments for Bascombe to assimilate the import of Patrick's words, and then Bertie ran after him. "I say, Pat—you cannot! You'll lose a bloody fortune! Take the Lyddesdale woman! If I am to be leg-shackled to Miss Canfield, you deuced well can take Mrs. Lyddesdale! At least she don't seem to be high-spirited!"

"I don't want her!" Patrick shouted from the stairs.

With a groan, Bertie sank into a foyer chair. A dozen thoughts floated through his mind and he didn't like any of them. Ten to one, someone would force a quarrel on Patrick Danvers, and the vicious cycle would begin anew. This time, he'd have to flee the country or face the ridicule of his entire family.

He was still waiting and still shaking his head when Patrick emerged bathed, shaved, and dressed less than an hour later. There was nothing in the viscount's manner now to indicate that he'd spent the better part of the day imbibing a large quantity of Madeira or that he was still in the devil's own temper. Only a certain whiteness at the corners of his mouth, the determined set of his jaw, and an uncharacteristic coldness in his hazel eyes betrayed him, and Bertie was afraid that a casual observer would miss the danger that lay shallow beneath that now calm exterior. Manfully he stood up to intercept Patrick in the hall.

"I am going with you."

"The deuce you are. 'Tisn't your affair, after all."

"But it is," Bertie insisted. "If I had not abducted Miss Ashley, none of this would have come about."

"Suit yourself then, but 'twill not be pleasant, I'll wager."

It wasn't until they were in Patrick's carriage that an even more disturbing thought occurred to Bascombe. "I say, Pat," he asked in the darkness, "but you ain't armed, are you?"

It was the first time in days that Patrick had smiled even faintly. "Alas, I am not. When I dispatch mine enemies, Bertie, I do it in the civilized way. And I have not the least intention of calling anyone out tonight, old fellow, because to do so would defeat my purpose."

Thus reassured, Bertie fell back against the squabs and stared dolefully out the window at the passing gaslights. It was late and many of the streets were nearly deserted, but he had little hope that White's would be thin of company yet. "I still think you could get Miss Ashley," he said finally.

"Do you truly think I would stoop so low, would act so dishonorably, as to steal another man's—even Rotherfield's—betrothed?"

"Oh."

Their arrival at White's was not unremarked. Even as Patrick handed his hat, cloak, and cane to the footman, there was a mild stir around him, a stir that spread as word traveled through the place that Devil Danvers was there. Play at the baize-covered tables slowed as he entered and stopped as he passed. A murmur of curiosity followed him through the rooms. Jaded gamesters long used to the vagaries of fortune merely looked up, while newer, greener young gentlemen just recently come to town scraped their chairs against the carpets and rose to trail a man they knew only by reputation. Bertie looked back in consternation and hissed to Patrick, "Carrion come to crow over your bones."

Behind him, Patrick could hear someone murmur in a low undervoice, "He's killed three men." His jaw twitched perceptibly, but his hazel eyes were veiled.

At one of the tables, Charles Danvers looked up and paled. Bertie groaned inwardly and hoped futilely that

Patrick would not notice his cousin. To his utter horror, Patrick made his way to where Charlie sat, standing behind him until he threw down his cards in disgust. "The luck's all yours tonight, gentlemen," Charles said as he pushed back from the table.

"Not quite," Patrick murmured above him. Taking a slim leather folder from his coat, he opened it and counted out one thousand pounds. Laying the sheaf of banknotes on the green wool cloth, he met Charlie's stunned expression coolly. "Your money, Cousin."

"Wha—" For several seconds Charles Danvers stared at the banknotes as though afraid to pick them up. "I don't—"

"It's yours," Patrick repeated. "I am settling the wager."

"Settling!"

Words were whispered covertly from table to table and then the entire room was enveloped in silence. Charlie's fingers crept toward the money slowly at first and then grasped it greedily. A perplexed frown crossed his forehead, creasing it. "But your year is not up," he protested lamely. "And Uncle Hugh—"

"I'll get my money back from him, but I would settle this now. Let us just say that I find it repugnant to have my name bandied about with that of every female unlucky enough to speak to me. When I marry—if I marry—I would not have it said that I took any lady merely to gain my fortune."

Charlie paled and beads of perspiration formed on his high forehead. The hand that held the money shook visibly. "But I have not—"

"I did not say you had," Patrick cut in coldly.

"I say, Danvers!" a buck of the *ton* protested loudly. " 'Tis not fair! There's men with money on you! Your time ain't up!"

"Aye!" several others chorused. "You cannot do it!"

"No?" Patrick asked evenly. "Ah, gentlemen, but I can and I have."

"But why?" someone behind him demanded.

"I do not believe I owe anyone an explanation." Patrick's eyes swept over the room, taking in the sea of disbelieving faces. "Is there anyone here who thinks that I do?" he challenged. He walked slowly toward the first protestor. "Do you, Kidwell?" There was an uncomfortable silence until the man looked away and mumbled that he thought no such thing. "Good," Patrick approved. Turning back to the rest of the gentlemen standing around, he fixed them with a disdainful stare. "I should dislike having to call any of you out for slandering any females of my acquaintance, of course, but I am prepared to do so. I dislike having my name bandied about also."

He turned abruptly on his heel and walked out between a crowd that parted silently to let him pass. A footman jumped to get his cloak, hat, and cane for him, and then brushed aside the coin Patrick offered him. Once outside, Bertie caught up.

"If you could have seen the looks on their faces after you left, Pat! You was magnificent!"

"No." Patrick's expression was bleak. "I was Devil Danvers."

21

The park was nearly deserted due to the early hour when Rotherfield and Caroline arrived. The mare he'd purchased for her was a sweet-goer, a pretty sorrel with a blaze, and it pranced stylishly. Delighted with the gift, Caroline put it through its paces and found it perfect. As she drew up from a canter, she leaned forward to pat the horse's neck.

"She's flawless, my lord. I can scarce thank you sufficiently, but you should not—"

"Nonsense, my dear." The earl took in her flushed face and the wisps of dark hair that escaped her chic military hat. "A pretty lady deserves a pretty mount, after all. And I must compliment Cecile for your habit —'tis charming."

She glanced down at the scarlet-and-black outfit with its frogged closures and polished brass buttons. "You think so? I feared to look like a remnant of Boney's wars."

"Not at all. In fact, you are a credit to me, Caroline. Even Ponsonby, who has quite an eye for ladies, owned I'd done it right this time. He complained I had stolen the march on him before you'd been presented."

Caroline considered the extremely handsome and charming Ponsonby and shook her head. "Spanish coin, my lord."

" 'Tis almost a quote, my dear. But do you not think you could bring yourself to use my given name, Caroline? I should hate to think we might be christening our firstborn before I ever hear you call me Marcus."

A rueful smile acknowledged the truth of what he said. "Marcus then," she managed with a lightness she did not feel.

"Good. I was beginning to fear that you would be like the Duchess of Wellington, whose conversation is peppered with 'my lord the duke' until poor Arthur is forced to escape to Mrs. Arbuthnot for comfortable companionship. Not that I should do likewise, my dear, for I expect to be a pleasant husband."

Steering him away from a discomfiting subject, she asked, "Are you acquainted with Wellington then?"

"We are not of the same circle, but 'tis not difficult to know him, my dear. He's not one to stand on ceremony despite the way he is lionized, you know."

She nodded. "I have even heard that he blacks his own boots."

"Remarkable what *on-dits* make the rounds amongst the *ton*, isn't it?" he observed sardonically. "I cannot vouch for that, of course. If you would confirm the rumor, you should have asked Westover—he at least served with him."

"He did not tell me—only that he was wounded and came back."

"I'm surprised he told you that. From all I've heard, he's remarkably closemouthed about the war. Not that he had anything to hide, but rather that he lost some friends, I understand."

"Yes—well, I would rather not speak of Patrick, if you do not mind."

"Patrick?" The black eyebrow lifted and the black eyes observed her shrewdly.

"Westover," she amended. "I should not like to discuss Westover. Now, Juliana—"

"And I should not like to discuss Miss Canfield, my

dear," he dismissed flatly. "Let us just close those chapters and let the book lie. The betting at White's appears to be shifting in Westover's favor since he has been seen with Mrs. Lyddesdale, and Haverstoke and Lady Canfield are both in raptures over Bascombe's engagement. By the end of the Season, I expect everyone to be wed and the maneuvering to be over."

"Yes—well, I daresay you are right," she sighed, "but—"

"No," he told her gently but firmly. "Have you given thought to going to Oakland?"

"No," she lied, when in fact she'd spent considerable hours pondering what to do. "Lady Milbourne is determined I shall be married from Milbourne House, but she is scarce up to the excitement. And Lady Lyndon is equally determined that it will be her house, so I have tried not to think of it at all," she answered lightly. "But we waste a lovely morning, don't you think? I shall race you to the corner if you will but give me a small lead."

"Done. You may have to the gaslight."

She gave the mare her head, fully aware that Rotherfield's big black would take the lead long before they reached the corner. And it did. He reined in and waited for her.

"Marcus!"

A nattily attired military man in dragoon colors hailed Rotherfield and rode to meet him. The earl looked up in surprise.

"Hallo, Major Thornton."

"Out early, ain't you?"

"Miss Ashley is trying out a new mare." Rotherfield indicated Caro, who'd just reached them.

"Delighted to make the acquaintance, Miss Ashley." Turning back to the earl, the major nodded. "Heard you was betrothed. Getting leg shackled at last, eh? Didn't credit it at first, mind you, but guess it's true."

"Yes. Caroline, are you acquainted with Major Thornton?"

"Saw me at the Connistons' party," Thornton reminded her.

"Of course."

An inveterate gossip, the major gestured for Rotherfield's attention. "I say, Marcus, you have any money on the Westover thing? If you did, you'd best be collecting."

"What?" Caro's world seemed to be spinning. "He got married?"

The major shook his head. "Latest *on-dit*—he paid up. Stupid thing to do, ain't it? Had plenty of time to win, too, by the looks of it. I had my money on the Lyddesdale widow—she wasn't afraid to be seen with him."

"He paid up," she echoed faintly. "But *why?*"

"Caroline—"

"Heard he was leaving town—someone said he was repairing to Westover, but then I heard he meant to go abroad—Italy, I think 'twas said. Not that I credit all I hear, of course."

"Italy!" she choked in dismay. "Oh!"

"I say, you all right, Miss Ashley?"

Suddenly conscious of the concern of both men, Caroline collected her disordered thoughts and nodded. "No—that is, I am fine, sir."

"You are certain? You look queasy. Maybe the ride—"

"Major Thornton, I assure you that she is quite all right, aren't you, my dear?" Rotherfield cut in as he reached to take her reins. "Overtired, perhaps, but otherwise fine. Indeed, we were thinking of repairing to Oakland ourselves for a quiet wedding."

"You don't say!" Thornton looked at Caroline again and tipped his hat. "Wish you happy, Miss Ashley—I do."

"Thank you . . . uh . . ."

"Surprising Season, I'd have to say," the major rambled on, "what with you and Rotherfield here—

caught the tabbies unawares, you did—and then there was Miss Canfield and young Bascombe.'' He shook his head in disbelief. ''Now, that was it, wasn't it? 'Beauty and the Buffoon,' Brummell calls 'em. Don't know how he gets by with it—the Beau, I mean—son of a tailor and all that, but he does. Heard he was in deep to the tradesmen, too—better learn to watch his tongue before he finds himself alone to face 'em.''

''I am sure that Miss Ashley has no interest in George Brummell, Major,'' Rotherfield interrupted sharply.

''Huh?'' Thornton looked up and encountered those cold black eyes. ''Oh, daresay she don't.'' When Rotherfield's expression did not change, he squirmed uncomfortably in his saddle. ''Well, best be going, I expect. Your servant, Miss Ashley . . . Marcus.''

''Pray do not let him overset you, my dear,'' Rotherfield murmured as the major rode out of hearing. ''He's a notorious prattle—nothing more.''

But she was barely attending. Her thoughts were on Patrick Danvers. He'd forfeited on his infamous wager and he was leaving London. Maybe she would never see him again. She closed her eyes for a moment to hide her pain from the earl. Well, she'd not expected to marry Westover, after all, so it should come as no surprise that he was leaving her life.

''Come, Caroline—I'll take you home. A little brandy and it will pass, I promise you.''

''No,'' she answered slowly, ''it will not.''

''It will,'' he repeated firmly.

''Poor Juliana—she cannot help hearing of Brummell's gibes.''

''That will be forgotten also. Learn to rule your life by your head rather than your heart, my dear—'tis less painful.'' He edged his horse so close that his leg brushed hers and the hand that held her reins clasped hers over the pommel. ''When we return from Oakland, I'll make a push to gain admittance to Almack's, and you will have the position you deserve. If you like, we

can leave tomorrow. I am sure that Lady Milbourne will
not object, and Lady Lyndon will be delighted to see me
in parson's mousetrap, whether she is there to witness or
no.''

" 'Tis so sudden, I—''

He nodded, a wry smile twisting his mouth. "All right
then—I'll not press you for now, but I mean to be
married before the Buffoon takes the Beauty, my
dear.''

22

Still unsettled by Major Thornton's gossip, Caroline managed to maintain an outward calm as she took her place beside Rotherfield to view the fireworks at Vauxhall. Clad as the goddess Diana in yards of draped white silk and thin-strapped white leather sandals, she found the summer breeze chilling. The earl noted her slight shivering and bent to pick up the shawl he'd brought. Draping it around her shoulders, he murmured, "You are lovely tonight, Caroline—the world will envy me the fair Diana."

The musicians played in the orchestra pavilion while a backdrop of lanterns glittered against the moonlit sky like stars. The fragrant smell of flowers and leafy arbors mingled with that of food prepared for a supper of arrack punch, powdered beef, custards, pastries, and wine syllabubs. Parties of young men and women wandered along the walks, admiring the fountains and cascades, and listening to the soft music. Billed in fliers as the "Garden of a Thousand Lamps," Vauxhall was a heady and exciting place.

Some distance behind them was the Dark Walk, and the screeches and squeals of imprudent females and Fashionable Impures could be heard as they were pursued by often inebriated young gentlemen. Caroline looked around her, noting who was with whom, and half-listening as a plump matron in front of her shared the latest Crim Cons with a companion. It was rumored that the Prince Regent was in attendance, but she didn't see him. Of course, at a masquerade, it was difficult to tell. For a moment she suspected a gentleman in scarlet domino of being Brummell, but then decided that the Beau would not condescend to appear in disguise. Turning her attention to the earl beside her, she found him absorbed in conversation with a gentlemen dressed as a Puritan. Marcus himself wore a plain black domino and mask with the resultant effect that he looked like Satan. The Puritan bowed and moved on.

"Would you like to walk, my dear?" Rotherfield asked. "We could go to one of the booths and get some punch, if you wish."

"I should not like to miss the fireworks, my lord. As much as I dislike admitting it, 'tis my first visit to the Gardens."

"They can be seen anywhere, Caroline, for they are catapulted into the air. Indeed, 'tis rare to sit to see them."

"Oh." She felt foolish, for common sense ought to have told her that. She rose reluctantly from her seat, very self-conscious of her Grecian gown and sandals and wishing she'd worn a simple domino instead.

Rotherfield read her thoughts. "Nonsense, my dear—any looks you receive will be admiration, believe me. But wear your mask if you are uncomfortable."

He'd been right, she had to own as they walked arm in arm along the scented walks, threading between the fragrant flower gardens and listening to the music. The night was pleasant, the stars were bright, and the lanterns sparkled like jewels around them. The orchestra moved from soft, pretty tunes to dramatic overtures, and balls of fire began exploding in the air above them, sending showers of shooting lights to fade just before touching earth. Had Caroline's heart not been heavy with indecision, she would have been hard-pressed to describe a more glorious night.

"Your thoughts seem to be your own tonight, my dear," Rotherfield observed finally.

"Oh, I have none, really—I am merely enjoying the beauty of the place." She managed to smile up at him. "You cannot know how I wished to come here, but there was never the opportunity. For years, I was with Miss Richards, and then Lady Canfield disapproved of masquerades."

"Really? Unless I am much mistaken, that is Miss Canfield over there with Bascombe."

"Perhaps now that she thinks Juliana safely betrothed, Lady Lenore is not so vigilant."

"Well, I should not entrust a female into Albert Bascombe's care under any circumstances." The earl's mood changed abruptly. "Would you care for that punch now, Caroline? There is Mrs. Farnsworth, after all, and I am sure you could wait with her while I join the line."

To Caro, it was as though he could not bear to watch Juliana. She nodded. "But I think I should prefer a syllabub, sir, if there is not too much wine in it." She continued to watch Juliana out of the corner of her eye and she could see that there was an obvious argument between the high-spirited girl and poor Bertie. She scarcely noted when Rotherfield left her side.

The words were heated and tempers flared. Finally Albert Bascombe left his betrothed fuming on the walk and stalked off. For an instant, Juliana stared after him in disbelief, then noticed the curious glances of those around her. Resolutely she positioned and tied her mask before pulling the hood of her silver-tissue domino over her blond curls.

"Females! Curst bunch of selfish, carping creatures, if you ask me!" Bertie muttered as he passed Caroline.

"Mr. Bascombe!"

"Huh?" He stopped and turned around. "Do I know you?"

" 'Tis me—Caro Ashley!" she hissed.

"Oh. Couldn't tell. You supposed to be one of them Greeks?"

"I am the Goddess of the Hunt—or so I am supposed to be."

"Look dashing," he offered gallantly, "but ain't you cold? I mean, your shoulders—"

"I *was* cold," she admitted. "Indeed, I sent for some wine syllabub in hopes of warming my blood." With a slight inclination of her head, she indicated where Juliana still stood. "I collect Ju's on her high ropes."

"High? Miss Ashley, she's a harridan! Fishwife's got a better temper, I can tell you! Wants me to cry off! Well, I ain't going to—fine gentleman I'd look if I was to do that. Let her cry off! She wanted to come to this damned place—for what, I don't know—and then she dragged me down some walk where females was getting kissed—and they wasn't all Cyprians, either! When the bucks started ogling her, I put my arm around her shoulder to protect her. You know what she did, Miss Ashley?" he demanded in aggrieved tones. "She slapped me! As if I ever wanted to kiss her! I'd as lief kiss m'mother!"

While Caroline watched, Juliana saw a man in a black domino disappear toward the Dark Walk. After a moment's hesitation, the girl turned and followed him. Caro, despite Juliana's recent outburst, felt a certain responsibility to keep her from ruining herself. And when she perceived that perhaps Juliana followed Rotherfield, she was determined to save her from her folly.

"Mr. Bascombe," she urged as she turned back to Bertie, "she's going to the Dark Walk—you must go after her."

"No." He shook his head obstinately. "Ain't going to—ain't making a cake of myself for a chit that don't like me."

"But it's not safe!"

"Let her ruin herself then," he muttered. "Maybe she'll have to cry off."

"Mr. Bascombe, at least you can come with me!"

"Me? No. Get Rotherfield or Patrick."

Torn between Juliana's imminent ruin and the information that Patrick Danvers was at Vauxhall, Caro clutched at Bascombe's sleeve. "Patrick's here?" she demanded.

"Saw him earlier—don't know where he is now. I say, Miss Ashley, but you're wrinkling m'coat!"

"Never mind. We've got to find Ju."

"Ain't going."

Throwing up her hands in disgust, Caro looked to where Juliana had been and there was no one. "Very well, Mr. Bascombe, I shall go myself."

"Can't—not the thing, for a female to go unattended. I say . . . Miss Ashley! Miss Ashley, you cannot!" Bertie called after her. "Females!" he groaned in exasperation. "Got to find Patrick!"

Caroline walked quickly, hoping she would not draw attention. When a buck stepped boldly in her path, she gave him such a look that even her mask could not hide her irritation. Taken aback, he moved to more promising waters. The place was not called the Dark Walk without reason—the lanterns were few and far apart and the place abounded with furtive giggles and whispered protestations. As she rounded a turn, she could hear Juliana's voice and she stopped short.

"My lord," Juliana pleaded, "listen to me! I . . . I have to tell you that I am not marrying Albert Bascombe—'twas all a stupid mistake! Mama contrived it! Please . . . I am not what you think me!" When he made no answer, she caught his arm and tugged. "Marcus, look at me! Oh, I know I am but a foolish child to you—but I think I love you! I . . . I cannot stand to see you with Caro! Oh!" Tears of frustration flooded her eyes and stained her mask as the man in the black domino stared at her.

Caroline moved purposefully forward. She'd given Rotherfield long enough to make a declaration and he hadn't, and it was time to spare Juliana further humiliation. A lump formed in her throat as she shared the girl's misery.

"Caro!" Juliana jumped guiltily and then jutted her chin mulishly. "I daresay you'll tell me I have ruined myself, but I had to see Rotherfield. I . . . I love him, Caro, and I cannot help myself . . . I—"

"Hush, love," Caroline soothed. "I meant to say no such thing, but if he does not return your regard—"

The man in the black domino disengaged his arm and reached to untie his mask. "As much as I am flattered," he told Juliana, "I regret you are mistaken."

"Ponsonby! Oh!" Juliana's hands flew to her face in horror. "Oh . . . my!"

Both girls stared at the handsome Lord Ponsonby. Mortified, Juliana felt the blood rush to her face. Caroline wondered how best to retrieve the situation. "My lord . . ." She stepped in front of him and laid a comforting arm about Ju's shoulders. "I pray you will not speak of this to anyone, for it cannot but injure everyone concerned. As you can see, she is overset."

"Well . . ." There was a twinkle in his lordship's eyes as he looked at the girl in the silver-tissue domino. "As she is masked and so are you, I could not be sure just who 'tis that loves Rotherfield, could I? All I could be certain of is that he's a most fortunate fellow."

"Ju! What the devil is going on here?"

There was no mistaking that voice. Caroline spun around and then tried to master the rush of emotion she felt at seeing him. His mahogany hair looked black and his eyes glittered in the moonlight as he faced the man in the black domino. "Marcus, she's a green girl, and I'll have you know . . . Ponsonby!"

"Alas, yes." The harried young lord nodded. "But tonight I wish I were Rotherfield if for nothing but the diversion."

"Your pardon, my lord." Patrick spoke in a calmer voice. "Needless to say, I should wish you to keep my cousin's name out of this."

"Patrick! He did not know me until you gave me away!" Juliana screeched in horror.

"Lud!"

"I assure you, Westover, my lips are sealed," Ponsonby hastened to tell Patrick. "I should not wish to quarrel with you, above all things." He deftly tied his mask back in place before bowing before Caroline and Juliana. "If you ladies will excuse me, I am late meeting someone."

It was then that Patrick became aware of Caroline's presence. Taking in her draped gown and her bared shoulder, he raised a questioning eyebrow. "And what are you supposed to be—Venus?"

"Patrick," Juliana cut in, "please take me home. I have quarreled with Mr. Bascombe and I have made a fool of myself in more ways than I can count. Please, I should like to go. And, Caro . . . oh, Caro, I am so very sorry!"

"Nonsense, my love," Caroline reassured her. "You merely spoke what you felt. 'Tis I who am sorry."

"You will not tell the earl, will you?"

"No, of course not."

"Ju, what the devil is going on?" Patrick demanded. "First, Bertie comes after me, telling me that you are going off alone to a place like this. Then I see you standing here like a watering pot with Miss Ashley and Ponsonby. He didn't—"

"Of course he did not. Lord Ponsonby is a gentleman, after all," Juliana retorted.

"He might not have known you were a lady," her cousin reminded her.

"What difference does it make now? I shall never be able to face him again."

"Well, I see you found 'em," Bascombe sighed as he came down the unlit walk. "Stupid thing to do, Miss

Canfield,'' he told Juliana. "Deuced stupid. And they say I am the slowtop!''

"Well! Do not use that tone of voice with me, Albert Bascombe! I'll—''

"Cry off?'' he asked hopefully.

"No!''

"Bertie, I'm taking Ju home.''

"But the fireworks ain't over—and the supper. Patrick, I'm devilish hungry!'' Bertie complained.

"Patrick . . .'' Caroline hesitated, at a loss for words. All three of them were looking at her. "Please stay.''

He sucked in his breath and nodded. "Bertie, take Ju back and I shall meet you at the entrance in a few minutes.''

"But . . . supper—''

"You can stay. Just wait with her until I get there.''

Once they had gone, Caroline could think of no way to begin. She felt as great a fool as Juliana. She untied her mask to see him better.

"Well?'' he prompted.

"My lord . . . Patrick—''

"You have the right name,'' he acknowledged noncommittally.

She could not bring herself to do as Juliana had done. What if he did not reciprocate her feelings? Lamely she looked at her feet and murmured, "I heard you were leaving London.''

"Yes.''

"But why?''

"I tire of the company. I am going to Scotland for a while to see my maternal relations.''

"Major Thornton said you forfeited your wager—about your fortune, I mean.''

"My, how gossip about Devil Danvers gets around the *ton*,'' he observed bitterly. "At least, this time 'twas gotten right.''

"You paid off? But I thought—''

"That the Widow Lyddesdale and I would make a

match of it? No—and when I found her name being bandied about in the clubs with mine, it was time to draw off. Why should I ruin the lady's rep with my own when I had no interest in that quarter?''

''But you had the time!''

He favored her with a sardonic twist to his mouth. ''I have ten months, Caroline. Assuming I found the lady, 'tis unlikely that even I could meet the terms, given nature's requirements.''

''Oh!'' She felt her face flush. ''But—''

'' 'Twas a stupid reason to marry, anyway. Do not be sorry for me, my dear—I'll come about without Uncle Vernon's money.''

''Patrick . . .'' She tried to bolster her flagging courage by stalling. ''Uh . . . how long do you expect to be gone?''

''Does it matter?''

She wanted to scream that it mattered very much, but bit back the words. ''Well, I was curious.''

''Truthfully, I do not know. Maybe a month—maybe longer. I may not come back until the Season's over. Listen—Ju's waiting. I'll take you back.''

She hesitated as he offered his arm. Then, resting her fingers tentatively against his sleeve, she started back. It wasn't until they reached the exit from the Dark Walk that she found the courage to pull back. ''Patrick, please . . .''

He turned to her. ''Please what?''

''I . . . I . . . Oh, Patrick!''

In an instant, he'd drawn her into his arms, and she could feel the heady strength of the man as he held her close. His lips brushed against hers and then he shocked her by taking possession of her mouth. She slid her arms around his waist and clasped him to her, savoring the sensations that coursed through her body.

When he raised his head at last, his voice was husky. ''Every time I see you I want to do that—and more.'' She leaned back in his arms and caressed the deep red hair at his temples before tracing the fine clean line of his jaw. The ruby of Rotherfield's ring caught the faint moonlight and reflected it into his eyes. Abruptly he pushed her away with such force that she staggered.

"What—?"

"Do you think me totally without honor?" he demanded harshly. "That I would dally with another man's wife? That's what you are going to be, you know."

"But—"

"Don't expect me to play Mars to your Venus, Caroline!" he snapped.

She stared at the glittering eyes for a moment, then ran past him toward the pavilion. Rotherfield waited, his expression enigmatic, as he saw where she had been.

"Your syllabub," he murmured when she took her place beside him.

23

A restless night of tortured dreams proved the final straw. Caroline rose early, determined to gamble everything for Juliana's happiness. As far as she could see, there was no good reason that five people should be unhappy rather than two. And, with that in mind, she moved decisively to put a fantastic plan, conceived of desperation, into play.

"My dearest Juliana," she wrote quickly, "I find circumstances dictate that I apprise you of the fact that I cannot wed Lord Rotherfield. I am firmly persuaded that we should not suit. Mr. Bascombe has reached much the same conclusion concerning his betrothal to you. And, while you are far too lively to be content with an amiable husband, no matter how wealthy he might be, I am not. By the time you receive this, Mr. Bascombe and I shall be on our way to Gretna Green. I am very sorry for the embarrassment this must cause you, but I feel that the result will be for the best. I remain, Your Obedient Servant, Caro Ashley."

To Rotherfield she wrote, "My dear Marcus, while I am cognizant of the honor you would do me, I have come to the conclusion that I could not be happy where I could not rule the roost. Furthermore, I suspect a sincere attachment on your part for Juliana Canfield.

Therefore, I think it best to end our betrothal before we are both unhappy. I am taking the liberty of removing Albert Bascombe from your path. By the time you receive this, Mr. Bascombe and I shall be on our way to Gretna Green. Your Obedient, etc., Caroline Ashley.''

Before her courage deserted her, she summoned Albert Bascombe to Milbourne House, and then she packed her portmanteau. Brief notes to Lady Milbourne and Lady Lyndon explained the true nature of her flight without any reference to Viscount Westover.

Proving he could read better than he could write, Bertie presented himself at the appointed time to find Caro standing in the foyer with portmanteau in hand. He frowned and drew out her letter. ''Was you leaving, Miss Ashley? Thought you wanted me to call.''

''I did. Mr. Bascombe, did you bring your carriage?''

''Well, I didn't come in a hired hackney, if that is what you are asking,'' he responded, still perplexed.

''Then would you be so kind as to take me to see my old nurse?''

''Beg your pardon?''

''Mr. Bascombe, it is imperative that I go.''

''Oh—daresay Rotherfield would—''

''Lord Rotherfield is inspecting a property today.''

''Then Lady Lyndon—''

''She is engaged with other plans, Mr. Bascombe. Please—after what I endured on the way to Calais, I believe you owe me this.''

''Well, daresay I do, but—thing is, promised to take Miss Canfield to a damned dinner party—your pardon —a deuced dinner party at Mrs. Chatsworth's tonight.''

Caroline suppressed a smile. ''I knew what you meant the first time, Mr. Bascombe.''

''Ain't far, is it?'' he asked cautiously. ''I mean, I don't see your maid or an abigail.''

''Lady Milbourne could not spare one, but no, 'tis not far.''

His expression lightened slightly. ''Daresay I could. It

ain't like I wanted to go to Chatsworth's, anyway. M'father's going to be there, and ten to one, he's going to want to know when I mean to set the date. But Rotherfield—"

"You will merely save him the trouble." She handed him the bag and proceeded to go out the door. "I see you have your grays."

It was not until he'd settled across from her in the coach that he thought to ask precisely where they were going. "Got to give my driver the direction, after all," he explained.

"Just tell him to take the North Post Road, sir, and we shall be fine."

"The place ain't got a name?"

"Yes, but I cannot recall it. I shall recognize it before we get there."

"Oh."

Caroline's letter to Juliana was delivered by a footman at almost the same time Bertie Bascombe's carriage left Milbourne House. Juliana pocketed it and slipped away to read it in the privacy of her chamber. At first, she could not credit it, but after rereading it a second and third time, it sank in that Caroline was not going to marry Rotherfield. Caro and Albert Bascombe. The very idea was so ludicrous that Juliana would have laughed except for what Caro meant to do to the earl. Rotherfield. How could he stand to know that his betrothed preferred the simpleminded Bascombe to him? Resolutely Juliana decided to put her own selfish desire for the earl behind her to save his pride. She would have to stop Caroline somehow—but how? She could not go to Rotherfield on the chance that he did not yet know of Caro's flight. Chewing her thumbnail, she considered and discarded a variety of impossible schemes, not the least of which was the purloining of her mother's carriage or her father's curricle—but then, she could not drive. If only she were Patrick. Patrick!

Heedless of the need for discretion, Juliana dropped

Caro's letter and sped down the stairs past bemused servants and out onto the busy London street. Running like a child escaping punishment, she traversed the entire six city blocks in a matter of minutes. When she arrived, Crump, Patrick's butler, stared in astonishment at the disheveled picture she presented and started to close the door in her face.

"I must see my cousin!" she gasped as she fought for air.

"I am afraid—"

She clung to the railing and tried to catch her breath. "You . . . do not understand . . . have to see him—'tis urgent."

"Are you quite all right, miss?" he unbent to ask.

"Ran from Canfield House . . . had to . . . Patrick . . ."

"Very well," he answered not unkindly. "You may come in while I determine if he is at home." But he'd scarce turned to find his master before Juliana was up the steps in front of him and on her way to invade Patrick's chamber.

She found her cousin conferring with Jenkins, his valet, as to his requirements for Scotland. Now totally out of breath, she could only grasp his shirt sleeve for attention.

"Juliana! What the devil . . . ? Jenkins, a chair! Ju, what ails you? Here, sit down and try to breathe easy." He took the straight chair from the disapproving valet and shoved it under her. Leaning over her, he brushed back her wild blond hair and mopped her perspiring brow with his handkerchief. " 'Tis all right, Ju," he soothed. "Just rest until you can speak."

"Patrick," she gasped, " 'tis Caro!"

"Caroline! What . . . ? Ju, get hold of yourself, girl! What about Caroline!" he demanded anxiously. "Is she in trouble? If Rotherfield—"

"No . . . no . . ." She shook her head vigorously and panted, "Ran away—"

"With Rotherfield?" His face had gone white in sharp contrast to the dark red hair. "No, by God!"

"With Bascombe!" she managed to choke out. "Patrick, she's bolted with Albert!"

"Oh, for lud's sake, Ju!" Relief washed over him. "You ran all the way here to tell me a farradiddle like this?" he asked incredulously. "I can assure you that neither has the least interest in the other. Jenkins, see if Crump can find some brandy for Miss Canfield, will you?" He turned to the valet, who was watching Juliana with fascination.

"But, Patrick, 'tis true!" Ju protested. "I had it of Caro! She wrote to tell me she was leaving with Albert!" Juliana colored and looked at the floor. "There is more to it, of course. Last night—when you found me in the Dark Walk—I'd gone there to see Rotherfield, to tell him I loved him . . . and . . ." She looked up to see the incredulous expression in her cousin's eyes. "Well, I do! But it wasn't Rotherfield— 'twas Ponsonby. Anyway, Caro came after me to save me from my folly. Patrick, she overheard what I said."

"That doesn't explain—"

"But it does! Caro's eloped to Gretna Green with Bascombe so that I may have Rotherfield!"

"Fustian! Ju, you read too many silly romances."

"But she wrote to me—I swear!" She dug in her reticule and then stopped still. "Lud! I left it at home. Oh, dear! Mama—"

"She said she was going to Gretna with Bertie?" The memory of his last encounter with Caroline Ashley came to mind. "When did they leave?"

"I don't know—she said they would be gone by the time I received the letter. Patrick, we've got to go after them! Rotherfield—"

"Hang Rotherfield! Jenkins! Tell Barnes to put the currricle to."

"Now?" the valet howled in astonishment. "My lord, I am not ready!" He set down on a table the tray he'd brought up and shook his head. "There's boots to be blacked, shirts to be ironed, cravats to be starched, and—"

"I'll be back—right now I am for Gretna!"

Jenkins stared from Patrick to Juliana in dawning horror. "Gretna!"

Juliana waited until the valet had gone down. "I am going with you, you know."

"No."

"Patrick, whether I like him or not, Albert Bascombe is my fiancé, after all. If we find them, 'twill not look so bad if we return together. Rotherfield will never have to know what happened."

He started to make an acid comment about the earl and then stopped. Putting his hands on his cousin's shoulders, he peered intently into her face. "You really do care about him, don't you?"

"Yes."

"All right then, but I warn you—'twill not be a pleasant ride, my dear." He dropped his hands and moved to a narrow cabinet. "There's no time to waste."

"What are you doing, Patrick?"

"Taking my pistol."

Lenore Canfield, on returning home from a trip to Gunther's, the pastry cook's, was apprised of her daughter's mysterious flight. Fixing Thomas, the footman, with a cold stare, she demanded awfully, "And where, pray tell, did Miss Canfield go?"

"I tried to follow her, Lady Canfield, but I lost her."

"Where?"

The footman squirmed uncomfortably and then blurted out, "Near Westover's, madam!"

"Patrick!"

Lenore spun on her heels and marched back to her carriage. "Take me to Viscount Westover's," she ordered imperiously.

When she arrived, Patrick's drive was blocked by an impressive black conveyance with the arms of Rotherfield blazoned in red and gold on the side. Lenore stepped down and marched up the stairs to where the earl was banging the knocker. Ignoring him, she waited for Crump to answer.

"My lord! My lady!"

Rotherfield and Lenore measured each other coldly before she stepped past him to demand, "I would see my nephew, Crump!"

"I regret that he is not at home, madam," was the stiff reply.

"Nonsense," she dismissed as she pushed him aside. "I have come for Juliana."

Rotherfield followed her inside while the butler threw up his hands helplessly. Jenkins, hearing voices and hoping Patrick had come to his senses, came down the stairs from above.

"Well?" Lenore demanded. "Where is my daughter?"

"Ahem." Jenkins cleared his throat and prepared to lose his position with Westover. "Madam, I regret to inform you that Lord Patrick has eloped."

"What?" Both the earl and Lady Canfield stared in stunned disbelief. Rotherfield was the first to find his voice. "With whom?"

"I do not know the young lady, but he said she was his cousin—Juliana, I believe he called her."

For the first time in her life, Lenore Danvers Canfield swooned. The earl caught her and carried her past the much-tried Crump to dump her unceremoniously on a sofa in the nearest saloon. There he delivered first a series of gentle taps and finally a resounding slap to bring her around.

"Control yourself, madam," he ordered curtly. When he perceived that she'd regained her faculties, he stepped back. "You may rest assured that I am going after them. I meant to speak with Danvers on another matter, anyway."

"Lord Rotherfield, I demand to go with you."

"Nonsense."

"She is my daughter, after all," she snapped, "and nothing to you." Then realizing that Rotherfield was virtually her only available ally, no matter how distasteful, she added in a more conciliatory tone, "Who can play propriety better than a mother, after all?"

"Very well then, but I warn you, Lady Canfield, that I cannot abide a harping female. One word out of you and I shall set you down on the spot and go on alone."

24

"I say, Miss Ashley—are you quite certain that we have not passed it?" Albert Bascombe asked anxiously. "I mean, we have been on the road two hours and more."

"No, we are not there yet."

"Thought you said it wasn't far."

"Well, I was not precisely sure of the distance."

"Miss Ashley, I am deuced hungry," Bertie complained. "If it ain't coming up in the next few minutes, I mean to stop at the nearest inn and eat. I didn't have nuncheon today."

"Neither did I."

"You didn't? Then I insist we stop. There's a place Patrick and me ate the last time we came up this road—ain't half bad if you like pork pie."

Caroline stared out the carriage window anxiously. It was growing late and there was no sign of any pursuit. Surely Juliana and Rotherfield must have received her letters by now.

"You all right, Miss Ashley?" Bascombe cut into her thoughts.

"Yes. I am a trifle tired, that's all."

"Thought you was. Trifle hagged, too."

"Thank you for noticing, Mr. Bascombe."

"Didn't mean it like that, Miss Ashley—assure you I didn't. Got no address, that's all." He stared into space for a moment and then sighed glumly. "You know, if a man had to get married, I mean, if I had to get leg-shackled, you are more the sort of female I'd take. Oh, I know, you cut up a devil of a dust at Dover, but you ain't given to freaks of distemper like Miss Canfield. If one of us don't cry off, I might as well put a period to my existence."

"Mr. Bascombe, you would not!"

"No," he admitted miserably, "but I ain't going to like being married to her."

"Perhaps it will not come to that," Caroline soothed.

Just then, they became aware of a curricle careening precariously close to theirs. Bertie's driver cracked the whip to pull away on the narrow road, sending the coach swaying. Caroline grabbed the pullstrap and looked out to see the door of the other conveyance mere inches from her window. Her eyes widened as she saw its occupants.

"Juliana!"

"What?" Bertie gasped. "No!" Pounding on the roof of the passenger compartment, he yelled above the din, "Pull into the Hawk ahead!"

The wheels brushed, nearly sending Bertie's carriage into a ditch. Caroline closed her eyes and prepared for the worst. Bascombe lost his grip on his strap and was flung into her lap. She tried to hold on to him with one arm as the other coach edged past.

"Are you all right, Mr. Bascombe?" she asked shakily when they were again on the road.

"No, I ain't! Of all the cow-handed things to do! Ought to be a law against driving like that!"

The carriage slowed and rolled into an innyard. Almost before it stopped, the door was yanked open.

"You fool! You bloody fool!"

"Patrick!" Bertie goggled. "What are you doing here?"

"Well might you ask," was the grim reply. "Pistols or swords?"

"What? Patrick, you've taken leave of your senses! Miss Ashley, you tell him—"

"I am afraid I left word with Juliana we were eloping," she apologized.

"No!"

"Are you getting down, Bertie, or am I dragging you out of there?" Patrick demanded.

Bascombe pulled at his cravat, which had suddenly become uncomfortably tight, but he managed to jump down. "Pat, it ain't—"

They were interrupted by the arrival of another, more impressive carriage, which came to a stop a bare ten feet from them. Both Bertie and Patrick had to jump away from the horses. A tall, hard-faced man stepped down grimly.

"Rotherfield!"

"Westover," the earl acknowledged. "I had hoped it would not come to this between us, but I cannot allow you to elope with Miss Canfield."

"My lord!" Caroline pushed past the stunned Bertie and Patrick. "Did you get my letter? Oh, dear—I can explain everything!"

"Caroline!" It was Rotherfield's turn to be shocked, and for once the usually impassive face betrayed a parade of emotions. "What the deuce is going on here?"

"I will be happy to settle with you, Marcus," Patrick interrupted, "but first I mean to deal with Bertie." His eyes met Caroline's for a moment. "As for you, my dear, if you could not stomach Rotherfield, you should have turned to me—at least I love you! I may not have as much money as Bertie or Marcus, but I'm not in Paupers' Row either!"

"Caro"—Juliana reached for her friend's hand—"I know what you would do for me, and I am grateful. I'm truly sorry for what I said to you, but—"

Caroline wasn't attending. A becoming flush had crept into her cheeks as she faced Patrick Danvers. "Is it true?"

"That I love you?" A wry smile quirked at the corners of his mouth. "Caroline, if I cannot have you, I don't want anyone." He opened his arms and she moved into his embrace. "Of course I love you—wanted you from the first."

"But . . . your wager . . ."

"Didn't have a thing to do with you after you refused me the first time. I never thought to collect on it, anyway. I'd have gone back to Charlie the day I made it, but I was too proud to let him crow." He cradled her against him and ruffled her hair with his free hand. "Lud, girl, but you've led me a merry chase—I thought I'd lost you to Rotherfield, that you wanted to be a countess. But then when Ju said you'd eloped with Bertie, I couldn't let you do it."

"Oh, Patrick, I do love you," she admitted mistily against his shoulder. "If you still want, I'll marry you."

"If I still want . . ." His arms closed tighter. "Aye—above all things."

"Very affecting, I am sure." Lenore Canfield pushed past the earl to face her daughter. "And now, miss, what is the meaning of this? I came on the information that you had eloped with Patrick. If you did not, then I demand to know what is going on!"

"Mama"—Juliana faced her mother resolutely—"I am not going to marry Albert Bascombe. You can send me to Crosslands to die on the shelf. You can starve me, if you wish, but you cannot make me marry him." Her eyes lit on her erstwhile betrothed and she shook her head. "And it is not because he is a slowtop, either, because I do not believe he truly is—he just thinks more slowly than the rest of us. What I am saying, Mama, is that I am crying off."

"I say, Miss Canfield!" Bertie brightened. "Deuced good of you to do it!"

"Juliana, you have traveled miles alone with an unmarried gentleman. If Patrick is to marry Caroline, and you are not to marry Mr. Bascombe, you are quite ruined," her mother announced flatly.

"Not quite."

In unison, they turned to the earl, who stood apart surveying the rest of them with a sardonic twist to his sensuous mouth. "Having just been jilted . . ." He looked over to where Caroline stood within Patrick Danvers' arms and nodded. "Yes, I forgive you, my dear, and wish you well." He turned back to face Juliana, his black eyes twinkling and his expression softening measurably. "To repeat, having just been jilted, I find myself available. If Miss Canfield has it in her heart to reform this miserable rake, I should be happy to take her off your hands. I suspect she needs considerable guidance that you are unable to provide."

"Marcus!" Juliana choked indignantly.

"Well, brat?" His eyes never left her face.

"I should like it excessively."

Lady Lenore opened her mouth to protest and then shut it. "Well, I daresay she could do worse. At least, sir, you are not a dance master or a penniless half-pay soldier."

"Exactly."

"And as for you, Patrick, I can only hope that marriage will put an end to Devil Danvers. The family has suffered quite enough." Lenore looked hard at her nephew and then sighed. "I might as well tell you, I suppose. Your Uncle Hugh has found a solicitor who believes that if every heir agrees, it is possible to break Vernon's will. You would receive only one-fifth of the estate, as it is to be divided per stirpes, or some such thing, but—"

"It does not matter, Aunt. As for your first concern" —Patrick smoothed Caro's hair affectionately—"I think you can safely say the Devil has met his match and is no more."

About the Author

Anita Mills lives in Kansas City, Missouri, with her husband, four children, sister, and seven cats in a restored turn of the century house. A former English and history teacher, she has turned a lifelong passion for both into a writing career.